The BLACK SIDE

ALSO BY COLETTE BLACK

MANKIND'S REDEMPTION
Noble Ark
Desolation
Mwalgi Justice
Lenfay's Hell (coming 2017)

THE NUMBER PROPHECY
Fourteen
Thirteen (coming 2017)

The BLACK SIDE by

COLETTE BLACK

Published in the United States by
Drapukamo Publishing
PO Box 21
Higley, AZ 85236

For Monet, who has the loveliest dark and twisted soul I've ever encountered. Thank you for making me laugh and helping me come up with the most interesting of my strange ideas.

Contents

The Art of Blood and Bourbon

"**So, what do you do** for a living?"

I cocked my head, studying the painting in front of us, sipping at my pinot noir. "I kill people."

Mr. Paul Browning did a double-take, a common reaction. We looked like we could be office mates, similar dark suits, dark ties, even the same shade of red shirt. He worked as an office flunky, only allowed through the door on his boss' coat tails. Of course, I was allowed everywhere. My line of work required I fit in, that I look like a man of his station. Other than my broader shoulders, two inches additional height, and my shorter-cropped hair, we could have been mistaken for one another, down to the same acrid brand of cologne shared by him and half the business wannabes trying to imitate those higher up in the food chain.

"I'm an exterminator," I said, taking another sip.

Paul imitated my action, gulping at his crass bourbon, ice clinking against the glass like a plea for escape. It still amazed me, the ease of manipulating others. Drink your own glass at the right pace, keep the conversation tense, and you could have a man finish a keg while you drank no more than half a cup.

His Adam's apple bobbed, an elevator careening to the rooftop before dropping to the basement. "I thought you people did your jobs at night." He gave a weak chuckle. "But I guess you can enjoy art like any other man, eh?"

I gave him a long stare. "We do our job any time of the day required."

I took another sip of wine, but he didn't follow suit. I gestured to the painting. "Interesting representation. I wonder at the title, 'Drunken Stupor.' It seems a bit off to me."

A crease of sweat at his brow, Paul gulped another mouthful of bourbon. "It's a guy passed out in a bar. Seems pretty straightforward."

Yes, Paul's IQ definitely fell below the new standards.

I pointed to the rumpled figure in the painting. "The slump of the body is unnatural. As if posed. The spilled drink, too red for anything but wine, yet the overturned glass still holds a few drops of amber liquid. The man is face down in his own blood. I would have named the painting, 'Stupid Drunk,' rather than 'Drunken Stupor.'"

"Why assume the man was stupid, just because he was murdered?"

I gave him a long look, took another sip of champagne.

4

"Right," Paul said, downing another long gulp, chunks of ice clambering over one another. "I guess to you it would seem that way, since your job is to rid society of the 'undesirables.'" Lines of sweat ran down the side of his face, the back of his neck. The man reeked with fear. I needed to calm him or he'd bolt.

I nodded. "That includes those with IQs below governmental standard."

Paul wiped at the moisture with the back of his hand, taking a relieved if somewhat labored breath. "I guess that makes me safe then. Are you here for someone else? Haggarty, maybe?"

I drank another sip. Paul downed the last of his bourbon. A thin sliver of remorse slipped into my conscience. I'd have that looked at during my next exam. A man couldn't do this kind of job if morals were allowed free reign through the psyche. Contrary to my usual restraint, the emotion spurred me to action, making me say more than I should.

"They raised the IQ limit," I told Paul. "You fell below. I'm sorry."

His face drained of color, the sudden spike in his heart rate finishing my job.

I turned to the exit, took another sip of champagne, and pretended not to notice the shatter of glass behind me, the tinkle of half-melted ice cubes dancing free across the tiles, or the thump of Paul's limp body impersonating the painting on the wall.

With a shudder--the only show of emotion I could manage--I drained the last of my drink, handing the red-stained flute to a waiter with a familiar face. He gave me a bland smile, as if unaware of my existence, though I felt his eyes follow me through the rotating doors and onto the sidewalk.

When my heart seized, pain shooting down my arm, Manhattan's high-rises and distant sliver of blue sky my sudden viewpoint, I realized the talk of upgrading exterminators' ability to repress emotion had already been initiated, but not on their men and women already in the field. My body convulsed then laid still, blackness closing in. Two heart attacks so close in time and proximity would seem unusual, but not overly surprising. People would go on with their lives, just happy it wasn't them...yet.

Author's Note:

The premise of this story has been with me a long time. Two people in conversation:

"Hey, what do you do for a living?"

"I kill people."

The shock, the inappropriateness of it all, everything about this opening scenario intrigued me. A few months ago, I finally put it into a story. I chose to place it at the anthology's beginning, because it's my personal favorite and the related picture worked well for a cover--a combination of favoritism and pragmatism.

Kairo's Opportunity

Voices from the outside world echoed in my hole, too distant to decipher. They sparked a vague genetic memory—dream-like images of two-legged creatures, coated in sheets of metal, carrying long spikes. Centuries ago, those voices brought fear and death.

I slipped my tongue into the air, searching for a change from the sewer stench in which I'd hatched. Nothing. No fresh breeze. No change in light. Only the putrid smell of feces, rotting foliage, and mangy rats.

I raised my head. There it was again.

"You'd better run, idiot. We'll make you sorry if we catch you."

The thump of large feet on hard-packed dirt followed.

The words were difficult to decipher, so different from the cadence and pronunciation I pulled from my inherited memory. But I understood the familiar threatening tone, similar to the threats of the two-legged animals—humans—who'd murdered my ancestors.

I stared at the small patch of blue sky shining between rustling branches of forest pine. I was meant for better things than a leaky pit of sewage. Deep down, my ancestors called to me, whispering that our kind were meant for majestic feats. Day in and day out, since I'd emerged no bigger than the smallest rat, I'd held onto that whisper, hoping for the day I could prove it true.

The pounding grew closer. Fleshy appendages wrapped around the wires of the grate, my only source of sunlight and clean air. Above the metal crisscross, a human boy appeared.

It grunted. Probably having a bowel movement. The smell from my prison often had that effect on animals, like they thought they could one-up the stench below.

But no, the boy was exerting effort against something, the grate perhaps. Like men had come for my ancestors, did the boy intend to skewer me with a metal blade?

Rivets popped. The grate's wires bent upward. The boy dropped onto the narrow ladder leading up to it, holding on with all four feet like a spider. To my surprise, he used a top foot—a hand—to pull the wiring back down.

An urge to defend my territory pulsed beneath my scales, but the human was big, three times larger than me. And those same protective instincts had killed my forebears. Maybe I should hide. But more reflection forced me to a braver course of action. If I ever wanted out of this filthy cage, I had to leave through the open grate before the human left and resealed it.

"We know you're around here somewhere, dorkus. We'll find you, eventually."

More humans. I needed to hurry. My belly close to the sewage bank's grime, I slunk to the ladder. My body straddled over the vertical bar as I wrapped the talons of eight webbed feet around every other adjoining rung. Step by slow step, I crept upward.

I'd nearly come level with the boy's head when he became aware of my presence.

"Oh my, oh my, oh my...," he keened, scrambling through the bent grate.

I crawled with him, using his back and arm as additional footholds. He screamed, as if fearful, as we exited onto the dry forest floor. He must have called for reinforcements. Three more of his kind stood waiting.

"Bryson!" The shorter, skinnier boy called the large one who had come into my hole. "You hid in the sewer? That is so—"

"What the hell!" said one of the other boys, picking up a sharp stick. "What is that thing?"

The skinny one took the weapon from his companion, pointing it at me. I shrunk against the side of a low bush, too terrified to move. The sunlit grass matched the green of my scales, the sun-burnt edges near the same shade of gold as the scale-tips, but it wouldn't serve as camouflage.

"Wicked cool! It's some kind of mutated snake, or a lizard or something. I've never seen anything with colors like that."

The boy poked its stick at my side.

I jumped away, hissing. My red crest-fan unfurled at the top of my head, a natural response that often frightened the rats.

"Look at that! It's like those crazy lizards in Australia or whatever."

"Leave it alone, Shawn," said Bryson. "Whatever it is, it isn't hurting anyone."

"Shut up, Bryson tattle-tell. I'm going to skewer it like a marshmallow."

Shawn lunged again.

I slithered to one side. The stick scraped my scales then bounced across the hard soil. My unwieldy body didn't move well on land, but I scrambled partway under the bush. The low branches didn't let me squirm any farther. I was stuck. Visions of noble dragons, run through with glittering shafts of metal, swum through my mind. This was a humiliating comparison, stuck through the back by a boy with a twig.

Before Shawn could finish the assault, Bryson shed a multi-colored outer layer of skin from his torso— clothing ? Throwing the soft fabric over my head, he hoisted me up and took off running.

Thrashing at the covering, my head eventually emerged into the bright sunlight.

"Oh crap!" Bryson said, glancing behind him. "Just don't bite me. Please, don't bite me."

I watched the boy, my inner eyelid moistening my unblinking stare. He had come to my rescue, so I would trust him for now. But I would keep a close watch.

We left the trees, our dusty path turning to a rock-hard black trail, a human thoroughfare of some sort. Ancestral memories told me we walked through a town, but the structures had changed since the time of my forbearers. A wagon the size of an adolescent dragon roared past. I squirmed in terror, but Bryson held tight and the thing ran away.

"It's okay," Bryson said. "It's just a car. It won't hurt you unless you run in front of it."

A little time later, we stepped onto a square of clipped greenery, one of many in front of identical human dwellings.

"Wow!" Bryson screwed up his nose. "I think you might stink even worse than the sewer. We'd better get you cleaned up before I take you into the house or Mom'll kill me."

I had to wonder at a parent who would sacrifice its own young, but the concern was short-lived. Bryson took me through a gate to an outside wonderland. A bitter-sweet smell emanated from a large pond of clean, blue water. At the water's edge, I wriggled from Bryce's grasp, falling into the cool refuge.

"Bryson Wilford Tell!" A woman exited the house, pointing at me. "What in heaven's name is that!"

She appeared surprised, but not prepared for murder.

"Hey, Mom." Bryce said. "I've named it Kairos, after the Greek opportunity guy. Isn't it awesome?"

∽◈∽

I rested my wide muzzle on Bryson's thigh.

Mom joined us on the porch, keeping a wary distance. "It's getting too big."

"She's not much bigger than the dogs."

"Neither is a crocodile. We don't keep those for pets either."

"She's nothing like a crocodile, Mom."

"Yeah, that's another thing. First, you say it's a lizard then it's some reptile I've never heard of, a skink? Now what is it? Four of its legs are gone, like some kind of guppy-to-frog, and it has growths all over its back. What kind of creature have we got here?"

I almost rolled my eyes. She didn't recognize a dragon?

"It has to go," she said. "I can't trust some wild animal, growing teeth the size of butcher knives, around my kids. And even in Wyoming, I don't think pets like this are legal."

Bryson made to argue, but Mom put up her hand. "I'm sorry. That's my final decision."

A buzz drew Bryson's attention. He pulled his cell phone from his pocket and tensed.

Shawn. I couldn't read the message, but by Bryson's reaction, he'd made another threat.

It didn't make sense. Bryson was twice Shawn's size. Why did he let the skinny boy bully him?

I gritted my teeth together, sharpening the tips. I could do something about it, if I ever got the chance.

⁂

With a dog leash wrapped round my neck, Bryson took me back to the woods. At first, I thought he meant to throw me into the sewer. But we diverted from the path, coming to a meandering stream near the forest's edge where he pulled the cording from my neck. He patted me above one set of wing knobs.

"I have something for you, before you go."

But I didn't want to go anywhere. I'd found a home, a friend. I didn't want to be alone again.

He pulled a bulging backpack off his shoulders. "I'm

hoping you'll know what to do with this."

Out of the shadows, Shawn stepped into the clearing. "I don't think so."

He yanked the pack from Bryson's fingers. I'd watched enough human television to recognize the weapon in Shawn's other hand. Where had the boy acquired a gun?

With a hiss and flare of my crest-fan, I stepped from behind Bryson.

"Holy shit!" said Shawn. "It's the size of a cow."

Bryson laid a possessive hand on my neck. "Give me my backpack."

"Huh-uh. I want my lizard back."

"Kairos doesn't belong to you. She doesn't belong to anyone."

"Well, I say it does. I had it cornered and you went and stole it."

Bryson's eyes went to the gun, the pack, Kairos. "I'll do whatever you want, Shawn. Just leave her alone."

"You're such a pansy. Let me have it or every day of your ugly life, I'll be standing around every corner, waiting."

Bryson trembled, but didn't move. Why didn't he stand up to the boy? Show him he was bigger, stronger?

"If you don't give him to me," said Shawn, "I'll shoot him."

I curled my lip, snapping my jaws.

Shawn jumped back, the shaking gun pointed at my head. "It tried to bite me!"

His enemy's fear must have inspired some courage in Bryson. "She's not going to hurt you. Just drop the gun."

I lunged forward, throwing my head upward and knocking it from his grasp. It skidded under a bush.

Shawn dove after it, bringing it around, his fingers too tense on the trigger.

Worried for my human, I threw myself between them.

It discharged in a wild array. Two bullets carved bark off the tree before he finally hit his target—me.

A painful sting bit into my back, but to my surprise, the bullet ricocheted. My ancestors' top scales had been impervious to humans' blades, but I'd never imagined they could withstand bullets.

"Aaah!" Shawn screamed.

I turned to see blood seeping into his pant leg, a minor flesh wound. The gun lay in the dirt.

Bryson scrambled around me, straining to reach the backpack.

Shawn wrenched it from his fingertips, hoisting it over one shoulder. "I'm going to call the ranger service on that monster!" He limped as he ran for the streets.

"He's got our dragon egg," Bryson whispered, following after.

I stared after them, stunned. Bryson had found another egg?

Though wounded and small, Shawn was fast. He reached the edge of town as Bryson caught up with him.

I tried following, but even with my increased size, I maneuvered better in water than on land.

Digging my sharp talons into the crumbling bark, I scrambled twenty feet up a large oak. From my new vantage, I could see Bryson reaching a hand out for Shawn's shirt. As he gripped the fabric, a flatbed truck drove by, laden with a few pallets of sheetrock. Shawn went down under Bryson's superior weight, but the backpack flew up, landing in a crevice between stacks.

I'd never tried this before. With a deep breath, I threw myself into the air. Flapping my three sets of wings, I bobbed like a drunken puppet. I careened head-on toward a tall juniper. At the last second, I managed to veer off, using my front legs to push from the branches. In fear, I released my crest-fan. Between it and my tail, I learned to maneuver. The combination of trial and memory, within a couple of minutes, had me soaring over the trees. I found Shawn, fists up, facing Bryson.

As I flew by, I roared. My empty stomachs gurgled, bringing memories of swallowed humans and burnt enemies.

"I've got this," yelled Bryson, towering over Shawn. "Get the backpack!"

I twisted away, searching the roads, climbing higher. Clumsy on land, I became pure grace in the air. I'd thought myself a water creature, but not anymore. The sky was my medium.

There. From the shadow of tied-down stacks, the black straps fluttered in the wind across the reddish-brown stone. I glided down, gripped it with my back talons, and rose high into the air.

Shawn was running again, going back into the forest. Bryson chased after.

I spied a rusted-out grill in the back of a deserted yard. A half-full bag of rain-soaked charcoal leaned against one rickety leg. I swooped upon it, clenching it in my adolescent jaws as my adult ancestors had dove upon knights and angry peasants. Paper and all, I gulped it down.

My second stomach rumbled. With a belch, dark

13

dust plumed from my nostrils. High in the air, I turned, racing to earth, an eagle sighting its prey.

Shawn turned to Bryson, gun in hand. Before he could level the weapon, Bryson kicked it out of his grasp.

My talons wrapped around Shawn's shoulders. He screamed. The smell of urine wafted in the updraft. Apparently, Shawn had a fear of heights.

"Put me down!" he shrieked, sounding a lot like Bryson's little sister.

Happy to oblige, I swooped lower and dropped him.

He sat in the shallow stream, relatively unharmed. Water broke around his shoulders, moving him inch by inch along the riverbed.

Bryson had shown Shawn that he could stand up to him. Now it was my turn.

Flying a dozen yards downstream, I flipped back. A few feet above the water, I flew toward Shawn, fire streaming from my open jaws. Steam curled up in a warm fog, filling the small valley.

"No!" Bryson yelled as I pulled up.

As much as he deserved to be roasted like a steak on a bar-b-que, I didn't touch Shawn. My fire continued down the river.

He escaped the warming water, but couldn't see through the mist. He set off blind, into the forest. It would do the boy good to get himself lost. Maybe he'd learn a touch of humility.

Once I'd landed, I waddled to an open-mouthed Bryson, leaning my head against his chest.

He wrapped his arms around my neck. "Are you all right?"

I nodded.

His eyes widened. "Do you understand me?"

I nodded again, trying to make human sound, but my vocal chords still needed development.

"Yech," was all I could manage.

"Are you trying to speak?" he asked.

I flung my head up and down, almost hitting his shoulder.

He stepped back, laughing. I dropped the backpack to his feet, nudging him.

"Yes, of course."

Both hands reached in, pulling out what appeared to be a brown and gray chunk of sandstone. I dipped my nostrils to it. They quivered with delight at the sweet, rust-like scent. It was a dragon egg, same species, male.

"You can't stay here," Bryson said. "Even if they think Shawn's crazy, they'll search these woods. They'll see the scorch marks along the river."

I touched the egg with my snout. "Wah,"

"Where? I've been thinking about that. I can only think of one place where you would be close enough to visit, able to hide, and have game to hunt so you can survive. Ever hear of Yellowstone Park?"

I cocked my head to one side.

"Fly north, during the night if you can." Bryson pulled a map from his pocket, showing me our location in southern Wyoming, and the area called Yellowstone Park in the northwest corner. "As you get close, you should be able to smell some of the springs and mud pits. It'll smell like rotten eggs. There will be warm, wet places, much nicer than a stinking sewer." He patted the egg. "Maybe you can hatch this baby."

Running a hand down my neck, tears collected in his eyes. I had no memory of dragons crying, but I felt the same moisture under my own lids. I'd never imagined it could be so hard to leave a human.

"You helped me stand up to Shawn. I don't know why I was so afraid of him, but I'm not going to let him bully me anymore. Thank you."

I didn't need mounds of treasure or a mountain fortress. Bryson's victory over fear meant more than a measly horde. And I had helped. *This* felt majestic.

I couldn't help myself. I stuck out my forked tongue, kissing him along one cheek. Then I vaulted into the air.

As I flew into the evening light, my future clutched in both claws, I knew I'd fulfilled my ancestor's destiny. Not because I had an egg, but because I'd accomplished what few of my ancestors had managed. From a centuries-old enemy, I'd made a friend.

On a nearby ridge, I spotted Shawn. He'd finally figured out what direction was what, but he had a very long walk ahead.

In August, 2012, "Kairo's Opportunity" won first place in the CopperCon 32 short story contest, judged by Ari Marmell, James A. Owen, and Janni Lee Simner. Their comments bolstered my confidence at a critical point in my writing career.

From Janni Lee Simner: "Just an all-around well-written story that had both solid craft prose and a satisfying story arc, and which felt clean and readable and really pulled me forward."

From James A. Owen: "I found very little to be critical of; reading it was like watching a talent show where a contestant is so good you forget you're supposed to be judging the performance. I ate it up."

"Kairo's Opportunity" was also published in the February 2014 issues of Sorcerous Signals & Mystic Signals.

Beneath the Skin

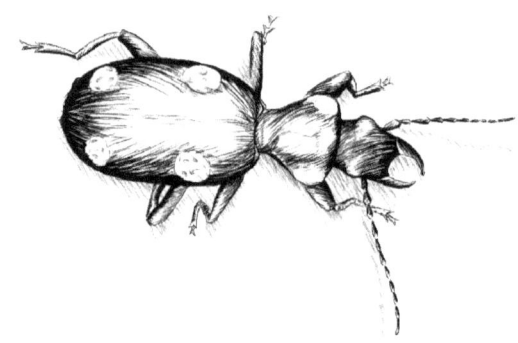

In the glaring afternoon sun, Kelley didn't notice the ordinary ground beetle; six white spots across its glossy-black carapace. Scientists would have recognized it as Anthia Sexguttata, though they would have been wrong and Kelley wouldn't have given it any thought, either way.

Escaping from the shadow of a rock, it scuttled quickly across the warm Indian dirt. Laughter drifted from the shade of a leafy, Sal tree. The other tourists, an overweight couple from Connecticut and two old ladies from somewhere in the Southwest, held lazy conversation while waiting for Kelley to finish her search.

The beetle reached her blue Nikes as she shifted her stance, bringing up her binoculars again. It stilled in the brown grasses, waiting.

"I think I see one," Kelley said. "Yes, look...between the trees down there. It's a big one."

Rahul Pradesh, her handsome Indian guide, chuckled at her girlish enthusiasm. "Ah, I knew you would be finding one. Bandhavgarh Fort is the best place in all of India to see the tiger. We have more here than any other places."

The beetle reached her shoe and climbed, latching onto her laces as it ascended.

Kelley placed a hand on Rahul's arm. "Thank you for suggesting this. You don't know how much this trip means to me, being able to see and experience India. I feel like a new person."

"It is my honor, Miss Kelley."

"Please, just Kelley. We're friends, right?" She smiled at Rahul hopefully.

"You haven't told me, Miss—" She frowned and he amended the appellation. "I am meaning Kelley. Why have you come here, all alone?"

She hesitated. "I just got divorced. My husband...ex-husband was a tightwad, but--"

"Tightwad?"

"He never spent money on anything that wasn't absolutely essential to life." The beetle reached her long gray hiking sock. "At least, so I thought. Apparently, his girlfriend saw more cash than I did. I paid the bills, but the money I thought was going to IRAs and such went into her pocket...or more likely, tucked safely between the surgically-enhanced hooters he gave her."

Though he probably didn't understand half of what she said, Rahul let her talk. Kelley was grateful for a quiet ear, someone to just listen, and not tell her what to do with her life.

Using its tarsal claws, the beetle carefully climbed the thick hiking sock, squeezing between the stiff folds of her jeans.

"I decided to take the settlement money and take

the vacation I've always wanted. When I get back, I'll be just another forty-something divorcee with no prospects and a dead-end job, but at least I'll have¬—" Kelley swiped at the back of her leg, clawing at the cuff of her jeans. "There's something...a bug or—" She screeched. "Get it off!"

The beetle dug its spiny claws into her skin, holding tight. In between each attempt to brush it off, it moved upward, in sight of its target.

"Calm. Miss Kelley, calm." Rahul placed his hands out in a placating gesture. "Just calm and we will be finding it."

She forced herself to stand still though her hands trembled. Rahul reached his hand up her pant leg. The man and his wife pulled away from the tourist group, slowly waddling closer with wide-eyed curiosity.

Kelley screamed again. "Ow! What's it doing? It's biting me!"

The beetle had arrived. It pushed against the soft flesh in the crease behind Kelley's knee. With clicking mandibles and sharp claws of its front fossorial legs, the beetle made a rough incision through the skin. Blood oozed, coating its hard shell. The slick fluid made it that much easier to insert its head into the small gap. Carving its way through the tissue, it squirmed forward.

Rahul's fingers clamped onto the beetle's slippery abdomen. "I've got it!" The beetle shot warm acid across the man's skin. "Aayee!" The blood-slick beetle slipped between his fingers, quickly pulling itself into the crevice between Kelley's muscle and tendon.

Rahul cursed in Hindi. "He got away. He is in the leg."

"In the...in the..." Kelley's eyes rolled up.

Rahul reached out with his free hand, unable to slow her fall. Her head hit the ground before her body pinned him to the dirt. Struggling to pull his hand free, he yelled behind him. "You! Mota—fat man from Conicut! Run down hill! Get help! She is fainted!"

The man's eyes went wide. "Me?"

"You see any person else? Run, mota!"

"It's Connecticut," the man grumbled as he toddled down the path, his wife huffing to catch up.

Rahul checked Kelley's skull. She didn't appear to be wounded, but he couldn't be sure. Did she have time to wait for help? He glanced at the old women, frail as dried leaves.

"I hope I'm right." Rahul hoisted Kelley onto his back into a fireman's carry, grunting with the effort. He was not a large man. Kelley, though thin and shapely, was not a small woman. He groaned, struggling down the path.

ॐ৻ঌ৶৽৾

Kelley sat on a mat of woven kora grass trying to come to terms with Rahul's words. Next to him, an old man squatted close to the dirt-packed ground, feet pulled in close to his buttocks and arms wrapped around his shins so that he seemed like a piece of folded paper. He had no shirt and wore an old-fashioned dhoti, like a dirty white robe, the long white fabric lending him an ancient air. His deep wrinkles, thick white beard laced with black and unsmiling face disconcerted her, but not as much as his crude suggestion.

Kelley stood and moved against the wall, away from the old shaman. "He wants to do what?"

21

"He says you are having a moon beetle in your leg. It has moved to your hip." Rahul pointed to his hip bone. "He says we must be removing it now, or it will be making you a night monster."

"A night monster? What do you mean? Is that some kind of Indian disease?"

Rahul shook his head. "It is a legend."

The old man gestured to Kelley, speaking in rapid Hindi.

Rahul nodded to the old man then turned to her. "It is said that the famous warrior from many centuries ago, Arjuna, grew haughty. He was saying that the men under his command had all power, greater than the God Vhnu and greater than the heavens. Brahma, the troublemaker God, created a small insect, something that could be crushed under a man's foot, to torment Arjuna and show his warrior's weakness. The beetle entered an unsuspecting warrior through the foot. Later, the moon shone upon the warrior. He transformed into a terrible beast, killing all of Arjuna's valiant men. Arjuna finally killed the beast then crushed the beetle as it escaped. Every hundred years, the beetle is born anew. It is said that Brahma helps it find a host whenever men must be reminded again of their weakness before the gods."

Rahul shook his head, lowering his eyes. "It is a silly story; silly superstition. Even so, you are needing the beetle removed. He will kill the beetle."

The old man slipped a sharp hunting knife from behind his rags of loose clothing. He mimed stabbing the knife, speaking again to Rahul in their chant-like language.

Kelley swallowed, suddenly light-headed. "Is he saying he's going to stab me with that knife?"

"We were wanting to do it sooner, but you woke. No worries. Madin is good with the knife—very quick."

"But he wants to stab me!"

"We must be killing the beetle when it is not ready." His fingers crawled up his arm. "It will be moving if it knows we are after it."

Kelley jumped up. "No way am I letting an old man stick me with a knife. It's only an hour flight to New Delhi. I'll find a doctor there."

Madin stood, speaking loudly and gesturing wildly with his knife. Rahul argued back until the man finally relented. "Be going back to America, crazy woman," he said in heavily accented English. "Take the monster to them."

Rahul ushered Kelley from the hut, tips of dried palm fronds scraping across her skin as if trying to hold her as she exited through the small door. The little thatched hut appeared incongruous among the mud-walled houses and richer cement structures of Katni. Usually the scenery, so mundane to the inhabitants, would have fascinated Kelley.

The beetle squirmed against her hip bone, sending a flash of pain that made her stumble. She grasped Rahul's arm. "Get me to the airport. Please hurry."

Rahul nodded, ushering her past a multi-storied apartment complex, the broken plaster creating designs across the sun-dulled blue paint, and into the resort's old jeep.

Getting a plane to New Delhi was the easy part. Registering at the hospital was like dodging her way through a carnival. She didn't have much time left.

Her flight would leave in three more hours. After much pleading with the attendants, nurses, and anyone else she could bribe, they put her ahead of the other patients and escorted her to a room.

Dr. Chatterjee, an older man with clean-cut salt-and-pepper hair and bifocals looked at her hastily prepared chart. "You know, Miss—"

"Kelley. Just call me Kelley."

"Miss Brown, I'm a general practice physician. I don't have any expertise in…" He glanced down at the chart, his brow furrowed. "Insects?" His Indian accent leaned heavily to British, giving him a condescending air.

"A beetle." Kelley swallowed. "It climbed into my leg." She could feel her panic rising. "It's living somewhere inside of me and someone has to get it out. Please, you're a doctor, right? You could put me to sleep, do an x-ray and find it. Please, I've felt it moving. You've got to get it out!"

"You think it's inside of you?"

"I can show you. On my leg." She tried to pull the leg of her jeans up, but the denim wouldn't stretch. In desperation, she pulled them off her hips, completely unaware of the doctor's wide-eyes and hesitant step back. "Look!" She pointed to the scabby wound "It climbed into my leg. Last night, it was at my hip. Some crazy witch doctor was going to stab me with a Rambo knife to get it out. Maybe I should have taken him up on it. A few hours ago, I felt something in my gut. Please. You've got to help me."

The doctor nodded knowingly. "So the village shaman frightened you with their superstitions—the were-beetle myth."

"But I felt—"

"Put your clothing on, Miss Brown. You felt it, because a part of you believed him. There are some types of beetles that can be quite aggressive. I'm sure one of them climbed up your leg, got stuck, and caused some damage, but I can assure you, it didn't climb into the tissue. Beetles, even ones here in India, do not behave in such a manner."

"But I felt it squirming into my leg."

"Even if it managed to do so, it would quickly die and your body acids would absorb it. I assure you, there's no need to worry."

"But—"

"I have many patients. I'm sure you understand. If you will take your paperwork to the secretary at the front desk, she can handle your bill." He stepped out the door and she was left alone.

Kelley stared at the wall. Maybe the doctor was right. Maybe she had imagined the sensation because she'd been so paranoid, so frightened. She glanced at a digital clock on the counter. She had two-and-half hours to get to the airport, through security, and onto her flight.

Gary McKeon, a forty-seven-year-old CIA operative finishing a London visit, stepped into the line of passengers making their way to the gate, heading for New York. A brunette woman, most likely in her early forties, stepped into line behind him, breathing heavily and sighing with relief.

"Worried you wouldn't make it?" Gary asked.

The woman nodded and smiled. "It's been a long couple of days. I just can't wait to be home, back on

American soil."

Gary noticed her t-shirt with I LOVE INDIA painted in bold red across her admirable chest. "India didn't live up to your expectations, huh?"

The woman shivered as if reliving some horror. "Just at the end. I'll be fine though. I'm sure everything is fine."

He hitched his bag higher on his shoulder, hesitated, then put out a hand, "Gary McKeon. If there's anything I can do...?"

They shook. "Kelley Brown. I'm okay. Just a bit rattled and eager to get home."

Gary almost pursued the conversation, trying to think of a way to get the woman's number. Even with shadows under her eyes and her long hair disheveled, she was a good looking woman. Based on the slightly off-color tan line around her left finger, she appeared to be recently single as well. The airline attendant took his ticket and ushered him forward. He'd have to find her in the baggage claim area after they landed.

⚜

Kelley found her seat by the window, wishing she'd had someone to pass the time with. Someone like the handsome man who'd stood in front of her. He was balding slightly but his dark hair and hazel eyes complemented a well-kept physique and easy smile. Instead, she had an empty seat between herself and an old woman knitting at the aisle.

Kelley pulled the window shade down as soon as she had secured her seatbelt. She didn't have enough energy to talk anyway, she told herself. She was exhausted, it was night, and she didn't want even the pulsing light on the aircraft's wing to disturb her rest.

A few hours later, she rubbed absently at the lump in her neck, below the surface of her skin. It squirmed. She startled awake. Screamed. With an open palm, she slapped at it, hitting herself again and again.

The old woman stared at Kelley, knitting needles poised. "What in the world?"

She pushed the assistance button, but it wasn't necessary. The stewardess had come running at the scream.

"Is there something wrong, miss?" The pale, blond-haired woman resembled a lemon in uniform. Her mouth twisted into a false smile. "Are you having a problem I can help you with?"

Kelley touched her neck. It had stopped moving. She shivered. She would have to find a twenty-four hour clinic as soon as they landed.

"I'm fine," said Kelley. She couldn't explain squishing a bug in her neck.

It took a couple of hours for exhaustion to overcome her horror. She eventually fell asleep with her head crooked awkwardly into the seat.

She awoke feeling rested and refreshed. She felt for the bump in her neck. It was gone. Maybe it had dissolved, like the doctor had suggested it would. She shifted uncomfortably in her seat, wondering if anyone in an American hospital would believe her any more than they had in India.

She opened the window shades. The bright light of a full moon hung large and overpowering on the horizon. Her skin prickled with gooseflesh. Her eyes widened; pupils dilating unnaturally. They expanded, pressing at her eyelids, burning. Pressing her hands over them, she tried to scream. Her breath caught in her throat. She convulsed. Pain shot through her skull.

"Are you all right, miss?" the older woman asked.

Kelley gargled, unable to respond. Her skin rippled across her back, like molten lead, reshaping and hardening. At the base of her ribcage, something pressed against her skin from the inside. She clutched her arms to her sides, doubled over in convulsing pain. The old woman pressed the overhead call button.

Kelley's jaw ached, stretching and enlarging. Two pricks of searing heat burned at the top of her head. Her buttocks bulged, pushing her forward. As the rest of her body pulsed and grew, bullet-sized spiracle holes opened from her hips to her underarms. Kelley could finally take a breath, but the air came not only from her mouth, but from the newly opened wounds along her torso.

The stewardess' shoes clicked against the plastic-coated runway. "Can I help you?" She glanced at Kelley. "There's an air-sickness bag in the seat-pocket in front of you." She sounded like an automated message, though she stood alive and in the flesh no more than three feet away.

Flesh, Kelley thought. Her mind withdrew as the beetle took control. "Flesh." The beetle spoke through her. The desire to eat, tear, and crush these large beings, always hovering omnipotent above, made Kelley's jaw twitch.

"Please use the bag if you're going to be sick, ma'am." The stewardess' voice was strained, thinly veiling her impatience.

Kelley uncovered her face, turning her multi-faceted eyes at the woman. "Human flesh." The voice sounded unnatural, raspy and deep, yet still Kelley's.

The stewardess screamed. Long antennae thrust

up through Kelley's dark hair. Large mandibles pushed through the skin along the jawbones like huge, reaching pliers. A pair of insect legs popped from the base of her ribs, through her t-shirt. Small spots of blood soaked into the white fabric around the new wounds. More dripped down her face, falling on her shirt and distorting the INDIA letters into strange blobs of red.

Kelley twitched her new tarsal claws, snapping her mandibles as she moved toward the stewardess. That high-pitched sound; it had to stop. Stepping over the older woman, either fainted or dead but blessedly silent, Kelley grabbed the obnoxious stewardess by the arm with one hand, her shirt with the opposite claw.

With one snap of her mandibles, the stewardess' head popped off her body. Her cries ceased, only to be filled with new ones; a disorienting cacophony of irritating noises. More than subduing the human beasts, Kelley wanted to shut them up.

A tall man with a scruffy beard and a large gut grabbed a flowery, china vase from his wife's Debenhams' bag. "Out of my way!" He crashed it over Kelley's head.

She screeched, frantically clicking her mandibles. The back of her jeans ripped and the point of her large abdomen protruded. Acid spouted over the man, forcing him to the floor where he writhed as the acid ate at his flesh. His wife shrieked, bending down beside him. Their noises mixed with the others. Kelley covered her ears, anger rising. Why couldn't they shut up?

Using her mandibles, tarsal claws, and her bare hands, she tore at everyone within reach.

Gary struggled through the people around him, trying to get a visual on the disturbance near the front. Whatever it was, people were in trouble. Cannibalizing a serving cart, he managed to pull free a twisted rod of sharp metal. His other hand grabbed multiple, blunt-edged, butter-knives. He forced himself over seats, through the clogged aisle, then froze. That beautiful, sweet woman. Why was he always attracted to the nut jobs? Kelley turned her large abdomen in his direction. Gary threw himself behind a row of seats. Acid splattered around him. A little girl's shrieking gained pitch. Gary peered over the seats. The girl's wounds were minor. Kelley's abdomen still twitched, but she'd used up her acid supply. He awkwardly jumped over two rows, jabbing at the beetle-thing with one of the rods, diverting her attention from the hysterical child.

Kelley's shirt tore, rising tight beneath her breasts. Broad wings spread from her shoulder blades into the airplane's confined space. She couldn't raise her heavy body much more than a foot, banging her head against the top of the compartment. But her timing was right. Gary's rod slammed into the flesh of her leg instead of her torso. She lifted her face and clamped her mandibles into the thick bulkhead. While her wings fluttered, she tore into the metal like she'd bored through flesh. He struck with the butter-knife. It hit her back, stopped by her exoskeletal forewings. Dropping to the floor, she ripped away a large chunk of overhead fuselage. Air rushed from the compartment. Oxygen bags dropped. The plane

30

jolted, descending toward the runway.

Lashing out, Kelly sent pieces of the overhead bins in a wide arc around her. Gary swiped at the debris with his weapons, unable to attack and protect himself at the same time. Something sparked. The lights died.

A toddler screamed in the walkway, staring at a woman on the floor, covered in blood.

Kelley took a step toward the young girl, mandibles clicking.

Through the plane's gaping hole, moonlight illuminated Kelley's disfigured form.

Gary slammed the sharp rod through her side, between two ribs. Warm blood soaked into her red-splattered shirt. She reacted to the wound no more than a cockroach might to a stickpin. She turned, ripping the weapon from Gary's hands. With a human hand, she grabbed the back of his head. Eyes wide, he thrust a blunt knife into her chest where her human heart should have been. Writhing in discomfort, her grip tightened. She placed her cheek against his, reaching her large mandibles around the front of his neck. Gary writhed, trying to find any weapon within reach.

A teenage boy in black goth, cowering between seats, handed him a chunk of thin, sharp metal, something Kelley had thrown aside as she tore the plane apart. Gary latched onto it. He stabbed it at her back, but only succeeded in scratching the base of her neck. Kelley pulled back in surprise, releasing him. Using the sharpest edge, he sliced the shard across the soft flesh of her throat. Blood spurted. In the seat next to him he spotted an abandoned knitting bag, needles peeking through the top. Grabbing one, he thrust it between the mandibles attached to her jaw, right through the pharynx to her brain. She convulsed, her strange glass-like eyes distorting, growing smaller, finally returning to their natural mahogany brown, then rolling up. Her blood-stained body fell from Gary's grasp onto the deck in front of the frightened, wide-eyed child.

The wheels hit the tarmac, the plane jolted and the spoilers flew up. The plane taxied to a special unloading area already swarming with official personnel. Gary stared at the dark-haired woman lying in a pool of moonlight and blood on the floor of the plane. The only evidence of what she'd become were the bloody holes at her head and down both sides, now looking like gunshot wounds, and a scraped-up chin. This was not going to be easy to explain.

Gary tried not to roll his eyes as FBI Agent, Martin Kern, stared at the blood-smeared body. The man didn't fit the typical FBI profile, at least how the public tended to view them. He was short and stocky, mostly bald with a swath of short-cropped blonde hair running a low circuit around his head. His pompous gaze shifted to Gary. "You expect me to believe the woman turned into some kind of human beetle and attacked everyone on the plane?"

"I told you, Klein. Everyone will corroborate the story. I know it sounds crazy, but—"

"Crazy? It's beyond crazy. What did someone do, slip LSD into the drinks? Put PCP in the air system? They did something, 'because there's no way that I'm filling out a report about a massive bug killing ten people and injuring fifteen others on a commercial flight."

"Identical mass hallucinations are impossible. Whether you like the report or not, even her injuries support the story."

"How can you tell with all the bullets you plugged into her?"

"I didn't have my gun," you idiot. He bit off the words, but he couldn't suppress his patronizing tone. "Look at the blood in her hair—that's from the antennae. Along her face and jaw; the mandibles— huge pincer things." Gary shuddered as he pointed out the rest of the wounds caused by her transformation. "You can see evidence of everything I've told you."

"Then why aren't they still there?"

"I don't know. When she died, she transformed back. I saw her when I boarded. She seemed tired, but otherwise—"

In the midst of their argument, neither man noticed the small bug wiggling its way from Kelley's ear canal. It limped, dragging a flattened right end, as it skittered across her cheek, six shining dots, like molten moonlight, across its back. It climbed from her down-turned nose onto the floor of the plane then paused, turning its antennae from one set of black, slick shoes to another. Neither man could hear the faint clicks and drag of the beetle scuttling toward its next target.

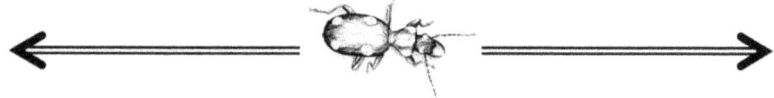

Author's Note
First published as "Becoming" in SNM Horror

Magazine, February 2011 issue, winning third place for best story of the month, it was picked up again for the anthology, Women Writing the Weird, published in October 2011 under the title, "Beneath the Skin." My next story is on the happier side, to get you over any creepy-crawly jitters.

In the Red

As Tiffany stalked to her bedroom, Andrea's adult tantrum echoed from the kitchen. *Two more years*, thought Tiffany, *I'll be nineteen, and I can request young adult housing. I'll finally be out of this ridiculous, simulated family.*

The white tips of her bobbed, rosy-pink hair fell in front of her face, a stark contrast to her dark skin. With a sigh she wedged the errant strands behind each ear, pressing her hand to the wall panel. The bedroom door slid shut.

"Lock."

Flashing words lit up the wall-console. *Door condition: locked. Access available to: Tiffany Contrera, Andrea Contrera-Stephens, and Ken Stephens.*

The only one not allowed was the one she might be willing to talk to—her little brother, Scott.

Tiffany popped a food pill, grabbed her calculus

assignment from a small pouch at her waist, and popped it in the one mm by two mm port behind her ear. She scanned the document for a full second then ejected it. The homework would take at least an hour, and it was the smallest of her assignments. She needed better enhancements, to sleep less than four hours a night, to work faster. If she didn't pull up her grades, the corporation might assign her to some menial-task job. But Scottie needed physical improvements to survive his athlete track. If he fell behind at eight-years-old, he'd never catch up. What Tiffany really needed was a miracle.

She pulled back her window curtains. That weird kid who'd moved in from the Moon's MiningCorp still stood outside his house, staring into the darkening night wearing black sunglasses. *Maybe...*

Reaching far into the back of her drawer, Tiffany's fingers wrapped around a thin dot about the size of a decorative sequin—a neural extraction download patch. If she got caught, school security would dock her for unprofessional conduct. But if she succeeded, she wouldn't need enhancers.

She pocketed the patch, the small gems in her pale pink manicure reflecting the overhead lights. She pulled back her drapes and slipped through her bedroom window, between fake bushes that smelled of dust, and across the street to Moonie's white porch. He sat in some archaic swing from who knows what century, making it squeak as he rocked back and forth.

Shifting the glasses atop his head, he grinned. "I wondered when you'd come over. You've been staring at me half the night."

"I have not!"

"You have." He tapped the glasses. "I've been watching."

"Binocular glasses?"

"Better than lame binoculars. I designed and programmed these."

"No way."

"Come here." He swept the bench next to him. "I'll show you."

Tiffany hesitated.

"I'm not creepy, just curious. You'd be scoping out the neighborhood too, if you had the equipment."

"Fine."

She dropped onto the cushion, whipping the glasses to her eyes. Andrea and Ken stood a couple of meters apart in their bedroom, both leaning forward, yelling at each other.

"Here." Moonie flipped a switch on the side.

The picture enlarged. Red lights pulsed on every octagon of Ken's nine-plex eye implant. Only the inside point remained steady, centered on his wife, while he diverted the rest of his attention to work projects.

Andrea was more invested; the steady lights of her six-plex pentagons crowded toward the center, like a glass fly going cross-eyed.

Moonie lightly grabbed her chin, tiling her head down. "Your brother is in his exercise room."

She focused on the slit of window protruding above the lawn. He had his hands out like a pair of fighter jets. The fingers jolted then crashed together. He simulated the finger planes crashing to the blue mat beneath his exercise equipment.

With Moonie's press of a button, Tiffany could hear Scott's flying, shooting, and crashing noises as he

37

replayed the scenario with slight variations.

Tiffany stared. "He's playing?"

Moonie laughed. "Every once in a great while, the kid gets a chance to be normal."

"Andrea has no idea."

"Of course not. You're only seventeen and you'd make a better parent."

Tiffany scooted sideways, letting one leg dangle and curling the other close. "So what's your story, moonie? Why is your family here?"

"My assigned name is Trykl Bashevis. I go by Troy. My dad was traded to DistribuCorp after my mother died." Troy swallowed, his pain obvious. "So, we came to live here."

"Were you and your assigned mother close? I've heard that can happen sometimes."

"Yeah, but she wasn't assigned. She and my dad are my real parents. MoonCorp used to allow that under certain circumstances."

"How barbaric."

"It isn't barbaric. It's natural. It's human. At least I have people who truly care about me. Or had."

Tiffany bristled. "A child doesn't have to be naturally born for someone to care."

"Of course not, but there has to be more to taking care of them than just getting an end-of-the-year bonus. Most of the adults here don't even look at children. They only see productivity quotas and dollar signs. *That's* barbaric."

Tiffany couldn't argue, especially with Ken and Andrea as case in point examples.

"I can help you finish your homework," Troy said.

The comment brought her back to the reason she'd come. The guy seemed nice, but a competitive girl had to make tough choices, for the sake of her class ranking.

"Really?" she asked, sarcastic. "Homework files are security-protected against any kind of tampering. It'll erase if I try to cheat. "

"I'm not going to help you cheat, though I could. I'm a computer whiz. That's the real reason we're here. Because of me, not my dad. DistribuCorp wants me for some ideas I've worked with. But on the side, I've developed a whole other world."

"Seriously? Like the banned sci-fi movies?"

Troy smiled widely. "You've seen a real movie? You must have some decent black market access. But come and see for yourself. I hooked up another interface."

His large palm engulfed her slim fingers, turning them warm. She didn't pull away. She didn't dare. Getting close to him accomplished phase one of her mission.

They slipped into his bedroom—more like a giant computer lab. The only space without consoles, wires, and wireless devices was his twin bed in the corner. Tiffany sat on it, leaning back and crossing her thin legs.

In a glance, Troy's eyes roved up and down her body.

She raised her eyebrows; part mockery, part invitation. This was almost too easy. A surge of anticipation and her heart beat faster. Just the challenge. Nothing more.

Swallowing hard, he turned back to his equipment. "I have to reconfigure the hardware and transfer program to take a new subject. It'll only take a second."

Tiffany waited, idly swinging her top foot

"Okay," he said. "I've got it."

Tiffany strutted close. Too close. He smelled of mint gum, stuffy rooms and teenage guy—that slightly sweaty smell that should be repelling, but reminds a girl she's standing next to testosterone.

"So what are we going to do?" She jerked her head toward the equipment. "Inside your little program?"

Troy took the hint and leaned in. "Whatever you want to do. But I thought you had homework."

"Is that all we'll have time for?" She let her lip pout slightly; an open invitation.

"I can make whatever time we need."

Troy touched his lips to hers. She'd expected it, but her own reaction took her back. His deep kiss drew her in.

She responded for far too long before she came to herself and remembered why she was there. With a quick slip to her pocket, she wrapped her arms around his neck. As she dug fingers into his hair, pressing her body against his hard, angular lines, she placed the small download patch at the edge of his cranium.

He pulled away, slapping his neck. "Ouch."

Tiffany laughed. "With all our technology, you'd think we could keep out mosquitoes. They're everywhere this time of year."

He shook his head and offered a weak smile.

Stupid moonie. Anyone else on the planet would suspect something, but as she'd hoped, he hadn't been here long enough to know better.

"Well, let's do this," Tiffany said. "How does it work?"

He pointed to a blue inflate-mat next to his computer. "Just lay down and I'll take care of the rest."

Despite a twinge of anxiety, she followed his instructions. She'd be vulnerable while she was under. Could she really trust this guy? Still, if she didn't go through with it, she wouldn't get the download and all her effort would be for nothing. She closed her eyes and tried to calm her beating heart.

"Relax." Troy kneeled down and pushed the hair from around her eyes. "I like this rose color. It gives you an anti-goth look."

She couldn't hide a slight shiver at his touch. "Goth?"

"A look some people adopted a long time ago. Black hair, black clothes, black around their eyes...everything was black except their pasty, white skin."

"So with my nearly-black skin and pasty everything else, I'm anti-goth?"

He kissed her lightly on the lips. "I think you'd look best natural, but still, I like it."

Tiffany suddenly felt guilty for the download patch. But it was too late now. You didn't patch someone then say "Oops, sorry. Didn't mean to suck out your brain." This was kind of on the unforgivable list.

Troy placed a cap on the crown of her head. "You'll feel a little prick at the base of your skull. It's necessary for the interface, but don't let it freak you out and do *not* move."

Before she could respond, the thing stung into her neck. She stiffened, despite his repeated admonitions to relax. Her vision swam. She twitched. The lights in the room blurred. Like a kaleidoscope, everything dissolved into a pinpoint of light then went dark.

Tiffany opened her eyes and gasped, then gasped again. She'd never imagined oxygen had a flavor, but breathing in the clear, woodsy air emphasized the polluted taint of her normal environment. Mountains rose to the east, covered with pine trees Tiffany had only seen in a forest museum. Aspens took more prominence farther down the hill and surrounding the small meadow where she stood. Past a meter-wide stream, the trees continued among the rolling hills with a smattering of fir trees, and small brush plants.

Tiffany stood barefoot in the thick grass, a flowing white dress twirling around her knees as she lifted her palms to the sky and spun in circles. Long dark hair fluttered across her bare, brown shoulders. She stopped, pulling at the long strands and staring. Her hair hadn't looked like this since she was five. Her skin was now her natural brown so her eyes had probably reverted to a sun-burnt copper.

She laughed, carefree for the first time in her life. What an amazing place…so open, so free.

Out of nowhere, Troy appeared. She gazed up at him, still laughing.

He swept her up in his arms and kissed her. Their light play from before had just been goofing around. This time, his intensity surprised her. His hand slid along the smooth skin of her back, above the low-swung folds of the dress.

It was several minutes before she reluctantly pushed him away. Troy tried to pull her back, but she couldn't let him win. "I have to get that stupid homework done. Whether I like it or not."

Reaching his hand behind her neck, he pulled her lips close. "We can do both," he breathed.

Considering what she'd done, the patch now firmly attached to his skull, sucking out his knowledge, she shouldn't be leading him on like this.

"Homework first."

He guided her beneath the shade of an Aspen where a large red blanket spread over the thick grass. "Relax and finish your homework while you doze."

Tiffany sat, leaning her back against the tree.

"Just access your homework through your implant like you normally would. You should be able to do the work faster than normal, plus we're already moving at higher speeds than in the real world."

"How long have we been here?"

"In the real world? Maybe a minute. I have a timer set. The computer will automatically bring us out in half an hour."

Tiffany leaned her head against the trunk of the tree and closed her eyes. Troy's hand traced lines up her leg.

"Stop that." Her eyes popped open. "I can't concentrate with your hands moving all over me."

"They're not even close to all over you. I could show you the difference?"

She glared.

Troy held up his palms in surrender. "Alright. I get the point. I'll go hike around a bit."

Tiffany longed to call him back, but she buckled down, retrieving her homework files. As always, biology came quickly and easily, but the computer applications were hard, tedious, and confusing. Though she managed to finish the assignments, she doubted the veracity of her results. She opened her eyes.

Troy stared at her, leaning against the smooth bark of an aspen. Though unusually tall and thin, his face was well-balanced, appealing in a way Tiffany couldn't identify. He didn't have the biological alterations of most of her classmates, made so the guys emanated sexual masculinity. But he seemed more real.

Her smile faltered. She shouldn't have placed the patch.

He casually strode to the blanket and sat down, leaning his elbows back. "So, what do you think of my world?"

She stared up at the blue sky, the wisp of a white cloud passing above them. How does one describe a foreign planet; a place only imagined, but never conceptualized?

"It's amazing. Where did you get such a concept? I mean, the food growing units open up the smog cover and let in sunlight, and there are mandatory sunlight centers at school, but even there, I've never seen the sky like this."

"That's because even the smog containment fields don't catch it all. This is the way your world looked before the pollution increases of pre-corporate government, maybe 1500 p.c. or earlier."

Tiffany laughed. "How would you know? It's not like we have nature pictures from p.c. time."

"You don't, but I do. I've hacked the corporate government files. They don't let people see what the world used to look like because it would create dissatisfaction. Dissatisfied citizens have low productivity."

Tiffany grimaced. "It always comes down to that, doesn't it? We have to be productive at all times, but I'm not sure I get the point. So we can have more stuff? Andrea and Ken are near the top of the power chain. They get bonuses, vacation houses, and they both buy or sell sex behind each other's backs on a regular basis. They don't seem any happier for it."

Troy wanted to kiss her again. "Wow, you really get it. It doesn't make them happier. The way people lived back then, when the world looked like this; committed to each other, to their families, and working to provide for one another. *They* were happy. It had nothing to do with how much stuff they owned, or the power they wielded."

"But wasn't the world dangerous? Like people died from diseases and stuff."

"Sure, but in the later years, with better medicines, those things didn't happen as often, and the hard things made them appreciate the good in life. They had empathy. They valued what mattered most."

"You make it sound so perfect."

"No, it wasn't perfect. That's what made it wonderful. A man and a woman had to work together to make it good."

"You wish you could go back in time?"

"I wish I could make this world real again. Corporate governments are getting more and more aggressive. They'll destroy the planet or each other soon. I don't want to be here when it happens."

He was planning something. Tiffany had no idea what, but the look on his face, the passion in his voice—he definitely had some scheme in motion. He reached over and ran his fingers through her hair. "You're really beautiful, you know."

Andrea had never seen a boy act like this. Sure, some guy might say she's hot, or put on moves to get close, but Troy wasn't looking at her like a new toy he'd like to play with. He was sincerely staring at her, at Tiffany, body and soul. But she'd only known him a few hours.

He ran a quivering finger down her neck. Staring

into his face, there it was again; such sincerity, as if he'd known her for weeks. But then, in a way, he had. He'd had those weird sunglasses within a few days of moving in. He'd been watching her, listening to her, for a long time. She should be mad at the intrusion, but she couldn't work up any anger. He knew the real Tiffany, not just the front she put up to survive.

Without meaning to, she reached her fingers into his thick tresses.

His lips clamped down. Within seconds, they slid down to the blanket, wrapped in a fervent, ever-moving embrace.

Troy cursed and disappeared. The world went black.

Tiffany groaned, opening her eyes. "I've got a soaring headache. Is it always like this?"

Flushing, Troy helped her sit up. "No. Usually you don't feel any different. It's probably because it's your first time."

He was hiding something, but Tiffany had too much of a hangover to care. She glanced out his window, framing her house's front walkway. Andrea stood at the sidewalk, hand on hips, all five taskers darting across their metallic pentagons.

"Oh, no."

Troy peeped through the drapes. "Andrea? She doesn't usually check on you so soon."

"Yeah, but she was mad. She probably came back to my room so she could get after me for not working faster. She'll go into the red if she knows I've been hanging out over here."

Troy grabbed Tiffany's hand, pulling her from his bedroom into the hallway. "You can slip out the back door, through the yards, to the end of the street. Then just go home as if you were on a walk."

As they passed the living room for the kitchen, Troy tried to block Tiffany's view of his father. The older man stared at the wall with sunken eyes.

Tiffany paused. "Is he okay?"

Troy shrugged. "He gets like this sometimes, since my mom died. It wasn't his fault, but he blames himself. He'll be better once...well, once I do some things."

She didn't press him for more, just nodded. She needed to get out of there before guilt pushed her into doing something stupid.

She placed a hand around his neck, retrieving the patch. "You're a good guy. I wish...."

"Wish what?"

She shook her head. "It's been nice. Have a good life and good luck."

He kissed her back. "I'm sorry."

"For what? You helped me with my homework."

"Come on," he said, leading her out the back door toward the street.

Despite a wave of overwhelming guilt, Tiffany pressed the miniscule dot against the edge of her skull as she left his yard. She didn't have much choice. If she didn't use the thing, the information would degrade within twenty-four hours. It wasn't meant to be long-term storage and the illegal little candies disintegrated once used.

Suddenly, the computer applications for her homework became obvious. She made adjustments to her assignments as she walked home.

Andrea waited on the lawn, hands on hips. "Where do you think you've been? This is exactly the kind of behavior—"

"I finished my homework," Tiffany said. "I think I work better when I get out of the house and move around."

She faced Andrea with a satisfied smirk. Tiffany knew acting superior to her supposed mom would hurt more than it helped. Andrea didn't deal well with threats to her authority, but Tiffany couldn't seem to help herself.

Andrea glared. "All of it?"

"Yes, and it's not only done well, it's exceptional."

Andrea crossed her arms. "Then send it in," she dared. "Let's see what kind of a score you've received."

Tiffany mentally accessed the files and sub-toned the send command. Within a few minutes both she and Andrea had access to the scores.

Tiffany walked away with her nose in the air. "I think I'll do my homework this way from now on. I don't need your stupid upgrades after all."

Andrea shook with rage, but her eyes focused on something else. A slow grin spread across her face. "You'd better keep it up."

Tiffany frowned. "So you can get your promotion?"

"Yes, and for your corporate future. Who knows, you could even move into management training."

"Oh, profit!" Tiffany exclaimed with mock enthusiasm. "I'm going to bed. I have a headache."

"Don't forget your tests tomorrow," Andrea reminded her. "Make sure you're ready."

Tiffany slammed the door. She'd be more than ready, for all that it mattered. Troy was right. They worked like slaves for some imaginary monster called productivity, but they never gained anything of real value.

She sighed as she lay back on her bed, imagining Troy's kisses and strong arms. She should have left the poor guy alone.

When Tiffany stormed across Troy's porch and through his open bedroom window, he was waiting for her. He sat at the edge of his bed, smiling. His arrogance flamed her fury. Because of him, her class ranking had dropped three places. He'd probably ruined any chance she had at a decent job.

Crossing the room, she swung at him.

Troy chuckled, grabbing her wrist. He swerved to one side letting her momentum help him spin her over his shoulder, landing her flat on the bed. He followed, stretching himself on top of her, holding both arms— now clenched in pummel-ready fists. And he kissed her!

That pompous, horny, thieving…. Oh profits, he could kiss. Tiffany stilled.

He let go.

She opened her eyes to that stupid, wide grin. Pummeling his back and sides, she made some good hits before he managed to restrain her again. "How dare you! You stole part of my upper-level biology knowledge. What a low, dirty—"

"I took some of your ability to learn, too. But it seems turn-about is fair play, you think?"

"What…" She flushed. "That wasn't the same."

"No. You didn't take my ability, just my knowledge. Not remotely alike. Although, I'm sure if you'd had the technology, you'd have taken both. You cost me a lot of time today, and caused an extremely embarrassing meeting with my supervisor." He paused to stare into her eyes. "But I forgive you." He gave her a peck on the lips.

Tiffany had to admit, maybe he had a point. "I received a horrible score on my endocrine system test today. Bad enough the computer applications section didn't make up for it. Andrea's overloading because it dropped my class rank."

"I really am sorry," he said. "But it is kind of funny. We both did it, both felt guilty, and we're both paying for our selfishness. Did I mention, I'm sorry?"

Tiffany couldn't suppress a small smile. "Yes, and I think you said something about being forgiven. I guess I forgive you, too. I was just so mad."

"I don't blame you. I was pretty upset at first...until the irony hit me."

Tiffany laughed.

Tentatively, Troy leaned down for another kiss.

It was several minutes before they pulled apart and Tiffany asked. "So what do we do now?"

Troy rolled off the bed, and put out a hand to help her up. "Now, I explain what I can of my system and we fix it."

"I thought restoring stolen knowledge was virtually impossible. Can you actually do something like that?"

"I could, if someone hadn't taken a good share of my computer understanding."

"Oh, yeah. That kind of messes things up, huh?"

He put an arm around her shoulder. "A little. It's okay though. You installed the upgrade you stole immediately, didn't you?"

"Yes. As soon as I left. I didn't want it to degrade." At least Tiffany had been smart about that.

"Good. I figured I could trust you to be practical.

So, the information is there. We just have to work together and find a way to fix what we've done to each other."

It took half the night. They redesigned the complex computer system, perhaps making it better. When they finished, Tiffany had her own surgically implanted port for the immersion cap. And they not only reversed the damage to one another, but managed to share the knowledge they'd stolen. The process had to be worth billions of credits, but neither one of them had any intention of letting the corporation know what they'd done.

Tiffany listened to Andrea's frantic tirade when she returned home, but even she couldn't dampen Tiffany's happiness. She'd easily surpass her fellow students and Troy would be able to carry out whatever plans he'd started.

⁂

Tiffany watched the funeral procession, shocked and embarrassed. Shocked Troy's father had committed suicide; embarrassed she'd had to sneak to a funeral in her school uniform. Not that she looked so different from everyone else; black and white made for a depressing theme anywhere. But the school crest of Profit Management Preparatory, PMP, emblazoned on shirt and jacket, caught peoples' eyes and their disapproving scowls. Andrea tried to ignore them, focusing on Troy.

With his father's death, what would happen to him? Would the corporation take responsibility for him, put him with another family, or stick him in a menial under-age job? She'd spent every spare moment with

51

him the last few days. Would this be her last chance to see him?

He passed, walking alongside the casket. He turned away from her gaze, hurt and anger in the set of his jaw. But why?

She received her answer as she left the chapel. Near the front door, an arm reached out from the maintenance closet, pulling her in among the auto-clean bots, computer controls, and cleaning fluids.

She reached for Troy, but he pushed her back.

"Who'd you tell?" he asked.

"Tell what? What are you talking about?"

"Suddenly the admins are playing hardball."

"Hardball?"

"It's a moon expression. It means they're getting pushy, nasty."

"What are they all worked up about?" Tiffany asked.

"That's just it. I had *them* worked up. I had them believing it was my way or utter failure. Something changed the balance."

Tiffany shook her head. "I didn't say anything, I promise. I don't even know what you have planned and no one, not even Scottie, knows I've been sneaking out to see you."

"Not even an accidental slip?" His arms were wrapping themselves around her waist again.

Tiffany gripped the back of his shirt in fists, pressing her cheeks against his dress shirt. "Unless someone can read minds, there's no way they could know anything."

Troy placed his chin on top of her head. His body tensed and he stepped back. "This whole thing has been a set-up. I bet we played into it even better than they expected."

"Who?" What was he talking about?

"Think. It's simple supply and demand. If you only have one person who can do what you want, and you want it bad, how much effort will you put into appeasing their demands?"

"A lot."

"Now what if you have two people? You think one is more suited to the task, but the other is more compliant."

Tiffany's eyes widened. "Then you can play hardball." She gasped. "They think I can do your job?"

"Yes," Troy said. "They killed my mother to get me here. Now they've killed my father, their leverage, to get me into their custody. If I don't work out, within a year or less they can train you to the job."

"The corporation killed your parents?" A week ago, even a few days ago, she wouldn't have believed it. But Troy had shown her hidden files. They would do anything to turn a profit.

Troy nodded. "I can't prove it, but yes, they did."

"What will they do to you?"

Troy scanned the closet as if searching for an escape. "Anything they want. To you, too, if we can't get away."

"Where can we run? The corporation has surveillance everywhere."

"Not everywhere." Troy stared into her eyes, sad but determined.

Now Tiffany's heart really did race. "You want to go into the other world, don't you? But you'd never get out again."

"We. I want you to come with me. There's nothing for either of us here now. And if they catch you, they'll force you to do the job they'd planned for me. It'll destroy everything, another apocalypse."

"That's impossible."

"DistribuCorp's CEO is crazy. Even a company shrink would certify him nuts if they could. But his plan might work. It would be the most massive hostile takeover ever. He would own everything or kill everything. I'm betting on the latter. And he wants us to help him do it."

Tiffany couldn't hide the quiver in her voice. "Could we ever come back?"

"I doubt it." Troy gripped her hands. " I'll take everything this time. Every essence that makes you who you are. Your body will become an empty shell left behind, like a wiped hard-drive, dead."

"We'll be safe there?" she asked. "Still alive?"

"Better than anything we have going for us here."

Tiffany couldn't believe she was doing this. She nodded. "How much time do we have?"

Troy cracked the door open and peeked out. "Depends on how far ahead of those thugs we can get."

Four men in dark suits, wearing security badges, stun guns, and immobilization gas on their tool belts, stood at the mortuary entrance.

"Easy," Tiffany said, pointing to the window on the outside wall.

It was just wide enough for them to squeeze through. Two security men in dark suits stood on the other side, watching the building exits.

Tiffany reached into her jacket pocket and pulled out some emergency school supplies—fireworks. "If we throw them into the corridor across the hall, the noise should bring every agent within hearing distance."

"How in corporate earth did you—"

"Same place I bought the illegal extraction patch. They're so old-fashioned most people don't even recognize them."

"There're no buttons. Are they remote?"

Tiffany reveled in finally knowing something he didn't. "Get ready to hurl yourself out that window."

She pulled out a thumb-size lighter and set it to the fuse. As it fizzled and sparked, she tossed the red bundle across the hallway into a perpendicular corridor. It slid almost ten meters. The hallway exploded with sounds like gunfire.

A couple of seconds later, Troy tumbled out the window and Tiffany followed. He caught her with both arms outstretched. Such a simple act, but in that moment she knew she was making the right decision. No one, fake parents included, had ever cared about her enough to even wait: not without tapping a foot, or yelling at her. It was a little thing, but it was everything.

They ran for the nearest hovercar— black, with SECURITY written in bold letters across the side. One of the idiots had been overconfident. His thumbprint was still signed in, the car on stand-by.

She and Troy pulled leisurely from the curb. As soon as they'd rounded the corner, Troy hit the accelerator, barely making it around the corners without losing magnetization and ending up stranded on the sidewalk.

Tiffany stared with guilt as they approached her house. She couldn't care less about Andrea and Ken. There was no love lost there. But she didn't want to leave Scott.

Troy picked up on her thoughts. It said something for how close they'd become in such a short period of time. "Where is he? Right now?"

"He should have come home ten minutes ago. He'll be in the basement practicing."

"Already? No snack, no…never mind. I should know by now."

Tiffany glanced behind them, tears in her eyes. "There's no time. I'm sure security will be here soon."

Troy took a deep breath. "Look, it's all of us or none, okay? I have the computer set-up basically finished. I'd prepared it for me and my dad, but I added another connection in case you wanted to come. Scott can use my dad's hook-up, but I need to reconfigure some of the algorithms. Get your brother and meet me in the basement."

"Basement? I thought—"

Troy screeched up to the curb in front of her house. "When I found my dad…you know…dead, I moved everything important behind a false wall we had put up in the basement. Come through the backyard. There's a green irrigation valve box next to the back hose. Lift it like a door and you'll find the way in."

Tiffany reached for the handle.

Troy caught her arm, pulling her back. "I know this is crazy. We haven't known each other very long." He kissed her. Short, but intense. "I love you."

Tiffany stroked his cheek. "I'll be there in ten minutes, no matter what."

"Five," said Troy.

She nodded, jumping out and running for the window-well ladder.

The security car flew through her neighbor's polyform fence toward their swimming pool. Somehow

Troy had disabled the car's proximity and occupancy sensors, sending the car off without him.

Tiffany entered her basement, nervous and worried her brother wouldn't want to come with her. He didn't even ask questions.

"If you're going," he said, "I want to come. I don't care where, just don't leave me here with them."

Tiffany hugged her brother and turned back to the open window. Andrea stood in the way, arms folded.

"I can't believe you would do this." For a brief moment, Tiffany thought their plan had been found out. Andrea tapped her skull. "They transmitted your truancy notice two hours ago. You can't just ditch school. It counts against your Networking Abilities Score. You're going back right now. We'll have to figure out an excuse for your behavior on the way. If we hurry, I can still get Scott to his enhancement installation."

Tiffany's thin fingers trembled against Scott's shoulder. "We're getting away from here. Get out of the way."

"Over my dead body. You have a responsibility to the Corporation, to the community, and to your family. I won't allow you to shirk your obligations."

Tiffany rushed forward, shoving her shoulders into Andrea's side. The woman side-stepped easily. She clenched Tiffany's upper arm in a hard grip, swinging her back. Tiffany's head bounced against the padded wall.

Even with her diminutive size, Andrea had so many physical upgrades, her strength went beyond normal parameters. And the multi-task implants made it child's play for Andrea to anticipate Tiffany.

One hand still holding Tiffany's arm, Andrea's other

hand clasped around her throat. "I've been waiting for you to do something like this. I've recorded this entire incident. I'll have you declared an Unprofitable Risk. You're going to—"

Tiffany's eyes went wide.

Andrea turned.

The base of a large lamp, appearing more like a baseball bat in Scott's unusually large and muscular hands, came down. A dull crack sounded as it slammed across the top of Andrea's skull. Her eyes rolled up as she slumped to the corkboard floor peeking from the edge of Scott's blue exercise mat. Blood ran in miniscule streams across the front of her face.

Scott dropped the lamp with a reverberating thud. "Did I...? I didn't mean to.... Is, is she dead?"

Tiffany knelt in the pooling blood, even as it started to seep into the porous cracks. She put fingers to Andrea's red-stained neck.

Her eyes raised to Scott's face—streaked with sweat and spots of blood. "It's okay, Scottie. I feel a pulse."

She didn't tell him how slight the pulse, or the likelihood the damage would still be severe. It wasn't his fault they'd given a little kid the power of a behemoth.

"What have you done?" said a deep voice from behind.

Tiffany spun to see Ken staring at the bloody mess, his square jaw hanging.

She grabbed Scott's hand and moved him through the window as she spoke. "You'd better call healthcare emergency. And we both know, if security shows up and thinks we're somewhere in the neighborhood, they'll order the medics to help with the search. It's more profitable. So you might want to give them the impression we're still in the house."

She glanced at the limp body on the floor, a deep sadness welling up inside. Andrea had been a lousy mom, but she'd still been the only one Tiffany had ever had.

"I didn't really hate her. I wish...."

She couldn't articulate the wishes she'd held as a child, the regret she felt now. She shrugged and slipped through the window.

Peeking around the house corner, she saw the security personnel had split into three groups: a contingent at the pool, some headed to Troy's house, and a few approaching her own front door.

Lights flashing, siren blaring, an emergency vehicle descended on the neighborhood, stopping in the midst of the officers. It drew everyone's attention, giving Tiffany and Scott the time they needed to duck to the neighbor's house and make their way to Troy.

Ken yelled from the front door. "They've attacked my wife. Please help me! They must be hiding in the house somewhere."

Most of the Security officers made for Ken, but not all. In Troy's backyard, Tiffany glanced through the slit of basement window peeking above the grass. A hulking guard tromped down the basement stairs. Tiffany froze. The man turned his head, his eyes widened, and he started yelling, going back up the stairs.

Tiffany saw the green valve box, almost perfectly camouflaged with the grass. She ran across the yard, tugging Scott behind her. The sound of combat boots on wood echoed from the front of the house.

She grabbed the lip of the casing and tugged. The plastic lifted, but didn't release.

The approaching stomps of multiple feet made the ground reverberate.

She tugged again.

Scott grabbed her arm, shoving her against the house. He lifted the trap door with one hand, the hinges at least a meter into the fake lawn. Tiffany had been standing on the slab of wood she was trying to lift.

The first security guard rounded the corner.

Tiffany pushed Scott down the dark hole, some kind of slide. She yanked the door to close after her as she jumped in.

A large hand gripped her wrist, jerking her shoulder, holding her suspended. The board banged against the guard's head, but he didn't flinch. His other hand grasped her forearm. He grunted, pulling her up.

Another set of hands, smaller but almost as strong, wrapped around her ankle.

"I've got her!" Scott yelled.

Troy's voice echoed up the chute. "Is she clear of the door?"

Scott climbed halfway up her leg, staring at the light streaming around her captor's thick biceps. They bulged, dragging them both upward.

Scott gripped his hands round the bottom of her shirt, bouncing as he pulled.

"Now!" he screamed.

The air crackled with electricity. A blue shimmer cut across the top of the hole. The man's screams mixed with Tiffany's surprised yelp.

She fell down the slide. Landing on top of Scott, the

security's severed arm fell across her back. The fingers still twitched, as if reaching for her.

Troy pulled her up. The tips of two severed fingers pressed against his chest as he hugged her close. Tiffany bit back the pain as it finally hit.

"Hang in there. Another guy's in the basement," Troy whispered. "You ready?"

She nodded.

He pointed to three spots, barely big enough for each of them to sit against the wall with their legs drawn in. He placed the cap on Scott first.

Having a needle plunged into his eight-year-old skull was too much. He cried out.

When he finally relaxed, his eyes glazing over, a knock sounded on the fake basement wall. Multiple boots stampeded down the stairs.

Troy grabbed Tiffany's face between his hands. "You sure you want to do this? We can never come back."

"I'll be more alive there than I've ever been here." She stared into his eyes. "Do it."

He placed the cap over her hair, inserting the needle into the access port.

Something hard hit the wall. One of the oldest of tools, but still brutally effective, a sledgehammer showed its ugly head.

The image swam. Tiffany gripped her brother's shirt.

Troy already had the computer programmed. He adjusted his own immersion cap, punching the enter key.

The head security officer's eyes glinted in victory at the sight of his prey. Their triumphant glow turned to fury.

Troy and Tiffany slumped into the wires covering the floor. He moved to grab them, but too late. All he'd catch were the three empty corpses the children left behind.

⊱⋅ ⊰

Tiffany awoke to a place she'd never seen before. Scott was laughing, rolling down a grassy hill.

Tiffany grabbed Troy's hand. "This isn't the meadow. Where are we?"

He turned her to face the small homes and fields.

"Don't worry." He pointed up the hillside. "The meadow is still up there, but it's not the best place to grow crops."

"We have to grow crops? But we're not even alive."

He pulled her face close. "Yes, yes we are. I converted our consciousness and we no longer have physical bodies, but in order to continue as we are, we have to receive power. For our human bodies, food provided that power. The crops we eat here are based on a complicated algorithm with the same meaning. We work. It creates sources of power. We consume that power to keep ourselves functioning."

"But—"

"Even if we didn't need it, I've studied sociological repercussions. We need work to appreciate life, to enjoy it."

Tiffany frowned. "Then what's the difference? All we did before was work."

"But we were working to meet company quotas, to have more stuff, and because that was all we could do. Now we work to provide for ourselves and the people we care about. We'll work alongside one another, and have time to enjoy being together."

A couple walked from the doors of a sturdy, log cabin. It took Tiffany a moment to recognize the man. "Your father? But how?"

"It's almost him. I had to improvise with some of my own patterns, but I already had his essential make-up downloaded."

"Then the woman is—"

"My mom, or as close as I could get."

Another couple exited the house next door. Several children showed up as well.

"I hope you don't mind," Troy said. "I extrapolated on your DNA to get an idea of what your parents would be like and any siblings we might have had. I added in some random genetics for a few other families in order to have a diversified gene pool."

"For like, kids? We're going to have babies here?"

Troy shrugged. "Eventually. But we don't have to."

She shook her head. "But I'm sterile. All girls are made sterile when they're fourteen. Re-population is handled exclusively by the PR department of the corporation. I never considered what it would be like to have children."

"Not anymore, Tiff. You have a choice."

Tears welled in the corner of her eyes. "We can have our own kids? They'll really be ours? And we'll raise them?" Her shoulders slumped. "I won't know what I'm doing."

Troy laughed. "As far as knowledge is concerned, we have every byte of information within a solar system network of computers to access." He pointed to a little red house with a bell on the top. "School will only take four hours a day. We'll download and store information at computer speeds. And don't worry, you'll be a great mom."

"A mom someday...I never thought...." Tiffany squealed, wrapping her arms around his neck. "I can't believe this! Thank you."

"Don't get too excited," Troy said, "There are a lot of changes to get used to. You might not like everything at first."

Her little brother approached, but different.

"Scottie?"

Troy put a tentative hand on Tiffany's shoulder. "I didn't have time to ask. This is how your brother looks without all the enhancements and genetic tampering."

Scott was still big, a bit broad in the shoulders and taller than most, but nothing abnormal. He grinned as he embraced Tiffany. "I'm okay here! Nobody expects me to be faster, or stronger, or better than everybody else. I'm just me and nobody cares. I love this place!"

He waved, jumping as he ran back to play with the other boys.

Troy pulled Tiffany's back to his chest, enfolding her in his arms. "We'll be happy here. It won't be perfect, but it will be better."

"For Scott, for you, for all of this..." Tiffany spread out her arms to the sky. "...it'll be worth any cost."

She wrapped her hands over his, leaning back and watching the wispy clouds on the horizon. They stayed, smelling the scents of flowers and trees, until the sun set behind the mountain pines.

Author's Note

My kids' overwhelming mounds of homework were the seed for "In the Red." I wondered at the section of our society that focuses more and more on achievement, and less on the joy of learning. What happened to neighborhood football? As the thoughts jumbled together, Tiffany and Troy came to life, along with the strange solution to their problems.

Eden's Hell

Gerard Fenacci's wince became a constant hunch of his shoulders. Their guide, a short Filipino man by the name of Miguel, decimated the dense foliage with something akin to avarice, his sharp machete severing verdant stalks growing between pine, banana and coconut trees.

Did the man have to clear a swatch as wide as an elephant? Had he no respect for the plants whatsoever?

Gerard ducked his tall frame beneath wide leaves, his dark hair catching on the uneven edges. Brushing it down, he pulled sticky strands off his neck, trying to catch a cool breeze. He couldn't wait to be done with this assignment and get back home, to his lab, where he belonged.

"I still don't see why you weren't in on this experiment from the get-go," Bruce Canard, a small edaphologist with wide glasses, said from behind. Sweat stuck his white cotton shirt to his torso even more than the rest of them. It traced streaks down his face and neck.

Gerard threw an exaggerated smirk over his shoulder. "Oh, come on Bruce. You'd have to live in a hole to be oblivious to the politics in this situation."

Bruce's focus on increasing nutrient availability in crop soils made him less aware of the botany side of the equation, but he shouldn't be that oblivious.

Samantha Grant spoke up from somewhere near the back. "Gerard believes all living things should be allowed to develop at a natural pace, without interference. They have a form of sentience and should not be trifled with."

Gerard was used to bantering with Samantha. It was all good-natured. Prettier than any female scientist he'd ever met, especially any from the computer technology department, she could say just about anything and Gerard wouldn't take it too personally. And unlike others in BioFuture America, she never let the discussion turn derogatory.

The BFA administrators, on the other hand, spoke to him with barely veiled disdain. Gerard kept expecting a pink slip despite his father's early years with the company and abundant contributions. But they stayed mostly out of his way so he continued his unorthodox research.

Gerard ducked the splays of a palm frond. "I don't know if sentience is really the right word."

"It's the word you used in your latest paper on the subject," Samantha said.

"You're taking it out of context. But they're aware. Multiple scientific experiments support my theories. Even the simplest layman knows if you talk to your plants, interact with them, or play harmonious music, they grow better. Sometimes the difference can be quite significant. My own studies--"

"I read the paper, Gerard. I don't need a recap." The good-natured humor behind the cut-off softened the sting.

He wished he could get up the guts to ask her to dinner, or even out for drinks. Maybe after they got out of this place….

Bruce slapped at a mosquito the size of a small fly. "So you really believe we're committing some kind of manslaughter or something when we eat a salad?"

Gerard laughed. "No. That would be like accusing a cheetah of murder when he kills a gazelle. But when we waste food, especially the way fat, gluttonous Americans waste food, that's blatant abuse."

"He talks that way," Steve's slow, deep voice boomed from the back of the line. "Like he's okay with eating meat and greens, but if you watch the man at lunch, it's like watching someone poke themselves with a pin. Guy's a wimp."

Gerard bristled. "I'm not a wimp, you oversized cretin. My body is in perfect balance. Unlike that mass of flesh you throw around like a sledgehammer."

Bruce edged closer. "Does it really bother you that much, eating the plants?"

"I've been experimenting exclusively on plant awareness since I graduated from Purdue fifteen years ago. The papers don't do my work justice. If you'd experienced some of the things I've come across, you'd have trouble with your salad, too."

Bruce shook his head. "Then I don't want to know."

"Most people don't."

They reached the edge of the compound, a giant chain link fence ridged with barbed wire. Devil's rope, they called the stuff in some parts of the U.S. Here in the jungles of the Philippines, it looked more devilish than ever, the sharp rusted strands curled between the fence and the foliage, strangling any plant foolish enough to grow within its reach.

Steve elbowed his bulk to the front, took out a key, and unlocked the simple padlock holding the gate shut.

"That's it?" Samantha asked. "That's all the security this top-level project warranted?"

"This is the outside perimeter," Steve said. "We have two left."

As head of BFA security, the board had insisted on Steve's presence despite his ignorance of the actual tests being conducted within the compound. To Gerard's way of thinking, he was there to shut them all up in case anything went wrong or they gleaned information the BFA didn't want made public. If Gerard had known Steve and his three goons would be joining them in San Francisco, he would have refused to board the plane back in Illinois.

The next gate stood within a perimeter of massive mason blocks. It was fingerprint coded, so Steve had to take some time entering in override instructions he'd received from administration. In the end, Bruce had to help him understand the more complex directions.

They stepped through to an enormous expanse of razed, black earth. Only a few, yellowish-green shoots peeked up through the ash.

"What could they possibly be thinking to eradicate so much plant life?" Samantha asked.

"Now you're starting to sound like me," Gerard teased. He frowned. "And in a way, so are they. They did this so the indigenous flora couldn't influence the plants within the area of their study."

Bruce shuffled uncomfortably down the dark, worn path. "Where are they anyway? The guards, at least, should know we're here by now, even if all their systems aren't working. Why haven't the scientists or one of their flunkies come out to meet us?"

Nobody responded. Worse than the lush jungle had hovered over them, slapping them as they passed, the empty stillness pressed their spirits down. The stench of death lingered in the air; not a smell so much as a feeling, like a cemetery on a dark night.

Silence reigned until they reached the last perimeter.

This fence rose in the form of an extensive electrical field. The schematics Gerard had glanced at earlier in the week suggested this wall—he'd assumed made of the durable plastic sheeting used on their greenhouses—extended thirty feet below ground, arcing upward into a huge dome. Water entered the area in the form of a stream ending in a small lake at the middle of the compound. The energy field hovered only a few inches above the running water which also contained a sophisticated filter covering every centimeter the shield didn't. The designers had assured nothing airborne or otherwise came in or out of the compound.

The group used a similar procedure here as at the last gate, a process replete with top-secret entry codes and passwords. When the electrical door opened, allowing two at a time into the holding area, they were sprayed down and sterilized. The sealed door dumped them two and three at a time into a giant Eden.

For the first few minutes, Gerard could only stand and stare. Stalks grew in wide, tall rows. Their massive husks, twice as large as any corn Gerard had ever seen, swayed unnaturally above their sapling like bases. Tomatoes the size of watermelons, ripe and ready to be plucked, fattened on gnarly, brown vines, similar to jackfruit branches. An orange tree, so covered in blossoms its greenery could hardly be found, rose like an oak toward the confines of the electrified dome.

Gerard shook his head in shock and wonder. "What have those idiots done?"

Bruce grabbed his sleeve. "Idiots? This is amazing! Can you imagine the production increases on even small fields? I mean a backyard garden could feed an entire family; maybe a neighborhood. Can you imagine?"

Samantha's eyes went wide. "Take a closer look, Bruce."

The small man leaned forward, squinting. "What? What are those splotches on the corn stalks?"

"Ants." Gerard answered. "Impaled by needle-sized thorns. I'm guessing they extend from the stalk when aggravated by climbing pests. Those beige insects drying near the silks of the husks were once corn earworm moths trying to lay eggs."

Bruce paled. "So the black dots around the tomato plants?"

"Some defense mechanism to kill the pests before they could bother the fruit, probably a gas or something toxic on the leaves. Every plant in here is armed to defend its seed. Even that giant periwinkle petunia some idiot obviously planted for fun, has thorns the size of a full-grown bougainvillea."

71

"Where are the scientists?" Bruce asked.

Gerard shook his head. "I don't know, but what they've done here is an atrocity. We should set the computers to annihilate the entire area before this becomes something from a B-movie nightmare."

"I thought you were into saving the plants, geek?" Steve said. "Now you want to kill them all? I don't have authorization for that."

Gerard glared at the small single-level structure in the middle of the compound. "This isn't right. They've taken their maniac ideas even farther than I expected." He made his way down the bare middle of an overgrown path that had once been three people wide. "Let's get inside and find those lunatics. They're probably hiding under their beds afraid to take responsibility for wasting BFA funds."

Each of them was again detoxed as they entered the lab portion of the facility, only to find a different type of inactivity. Equipment sat out as if in the midst of experiments. A microscope light shone on a prepared slide. A lab shaker oscillated, sloshing a number of beakers filled with gooey green liquid back and forth on its wide table.

The hum of computers, buzz of equipment, and the persistent swill of the chlorophyll sludge pierced the silence. This was nothing and yet everything like the razed ground near the entrance. Gerard found this scenario much more disturbing. The scientists weren't hiding. One way or another, they weren't here.

"Steve, take your goons," Gerard said. "Investigate farther into the facility. See if there are any survivors."

"Survivors?" Bruce gulped. "You think—"

Steve folded his bulging arms across his stomach. "You're not in charge, Fenacci. Davis gave me responsibility for this assignment, because he knew you'd do something stupid."

"I don't really care. I'm going to do what needs to be done. Stand there or look around. I'm here to analyze data. You can explain to your superiors where, in this facility the size of a peanut, their prize scientists could have disappeared."

Gerardo sat down at the nearest computer, punching in pass codes nobody had bothered to give Steve. They wouldn't have done him any good.

Samantha sat beside him at the adjoining computer. "I'll help you sift through the files, find those pertinent to recent activity."

Bruce pulled at his shirt. "It's almost as stuffy in here as outside. Any chance someone could service the filtering system, see if we can get some fresh air blowing?"

Steve grunted, ordering a couple of his guys to take care of the ventilation system at the back of the building. He directed the other one to follow him toward the living quarters.

Gerard glanced up before everyone was out of earshot. "Since Steve won't say it, I will. Use the short-distance communication devices the company gave us and stay in touch. Something is going on here and it might take a while to figure it out."

Steve scowled, but nodded as he went down the narrow corridor, tapping the black contraption wrapped around the back of his ear.

"What would you like me to do?" Miguel asked.

Gerard had nearly forgotten the small guide. "Just keep an eye out while we do our work."

Gerard accessed the computer systems and started searching through the data files.

After twiddling his fingers for a while, Bruce rose from his stool in the corner. "I'm going to go see how the maintenance guy is doing. It seems to be taking him a while just to change out a few filters."

Gerard barely nodded, focused on the files showing the genetic changes they'd been attempting on the plants—resistant to disease and pests yet harvestable by big machinery. These weren't meant to go in grandma's raised bed on the back porch. He moved ahead into a complex genetic analysis of the new hybrids.

Bruce's voice came through Gerard's earpiece. "Wow, these are the filthiest filters I've ever seen. All three layers are covered in muck. I can't believe we can even breathe in here. The guy has one more to switch out then we can have--"

Steve's voice broke over Gerard's. "The rooms have all been empty so far. There's only one left, but our codes aren't working to get it open. We're going to see if we can force our way in."

Gerard opened the clinical observation file. The data, comprised of every visual study, including video in real and sped-up time, along with the botanist's evaluations, filled the file.

Samantha stepped away from their screen. "I'll go give Steve a hand before he irretrievably breaks something even I can't fix."

Gerard didn't hear or notice. His attention focused on one real-time video encompassing the petunias and the tomatoes. He brought up several windows outlining the DNA structure of both plants.

This can't be. It's not possible, not on this scale.

"Everybody get back here immediately!" Gerard yelled. "I don't' care what you're doing or what you have to drop."

"But we're almost--" said Bruce. "What the hell?"

A loud crash sounded from the living quarters. Gerard threw his chair back, running to the end of the corridor. Miguel followed.

Samantha must have listened, making her way back like Gerard had asked. She was only a few meters from the lab, at the corner where the hallway turned toward living quarters. She was facing the sound at the other end of the corridor, where Steve had been breaking down one of the doors. Eyes wide, her face drained of color. She screamed. Backing into the wall, she screamed over and over again.

Gerard rushed forward, pulling her away.

She stumbled as she ran with him, stammering and sobbing, unable to form words.

Gerard yanked at a closet door marked Biohazard Emergencies. Pulling out yellow hazmat suit bundles he threw one to Miguel, still wide-eyed and confused. Before Samantha could take hers, she hurled the contents of her stomach across the floor.

Gerard hauled her upright. "I'm sorry, but we don't have time for that. Get this thing on."

He started dressing her, until her trembling fingers gained control and she began fitting herself. Gerard had just started with his own when Bruce tumbled around the corner. Not waiting for him to reach them, Gerard threw another bundle across the room.

Bruce hurriedly pulled on the suit, but he was a few seconds behind the rest of them. The guy babbled out of control as he went. Nobody could understand him, but everyone besides Miguel knew what those mutant growths from the compound could do.

Bruce finished zipping the suit. He only needed to

pull the fireman-style safety boots over the other layers then they'd be ready to go. He screamed in sudden pain.

"No! It can't! Please...." He screamed again, dropping on his side to the floor.

Gerard reached out to him, but Samantha pulled him back. "You don't want to get close to one of those things."

Bruce contorted on the floor for a few more seconds then fell onto his back, completely silent.

The suit continued to crinkle as it bulged and moved. Through the communication link Gerard heard squelching, snapping, and sliding movement similar to writhing snakes. It wasn't until green tendrils shot from Bruce's vacant eyes, out from his ear canal, that Gerard fully believed what he already knew.

Within seconds, the entire bone structure of the man's face fell apart, decomposed to nothing but skull and flaccid equipment. Broad green leaves pressed his broken glasses against the surface of the hazmat's faceplate. The plastic lenses scratched across the surface, making pulsing movements, cracking into shards. Before the plant could escape through the thick faceplate, green stalks pushed the yellow booties from Bruce's feet. Reaching upward toward the fluorescent lights of the lab, it grew less than a foot before a bulbous bud formed, exploding into a wide periwinkle petunia with blood-red veins.

Gerard shook away his morbid fascination, ushering Miguel and Samantha into the detox chamber as the blossom browned, curled up on itself, and seemed to die. The calyx left behind swelled like the womb of some withered old woman suddenly teeming with life. As the chamber doors closed, it burst, throwing hundreds, maybe thousands, of fat black seeds the size of peppercorns into the air. Several clattered onto the floor of the chamber and bounced against the sealing doors.

Miguel slumped to his knees, crossing himself, and repeating words in his native Ilokano dialect over and over again. It sounded like "apple juice," but was probably a prayer of some sort.

Gerard pressed the detox button, the spray not only sterilizing the suits from germs, but according to the information he'd read on the computer, it contained human-safe pesticides and herbicides as well. The seeds washed down the drain along with the chemicals.

Gerard breathed a sigh of relief. "We're safe for now. Let's take a little breather then we've got to make it across the yard to the gate."

"What's happening?" Samantha cried. "Steve burst through the door in the hallway then tomato plants were growing all over him. They didn't even have time to scream. This can't be possible!"

Gerard tried to put an arm around her shoulders. It didn't work well with the suits, but it was an attempt. "Were there plants behind the door?"

"Not live ones. A withered dead one was just inside, but it fell apart when Steve forced the door."

Gerard shook his head. "He dispersed the seeds. They landed on living tissue and immediately germinated."

"Plants can't do that, especially not on people!"

"Why not? We have moisture and nutrients. Break through the skin and we're a virtual smorgasbord of palatable, carnivorous, plant food."

Miguel continued his rocking motion. He clutched

at the chest of his suit, presumably where his cross would be, and repeated his mantra. Gerard finally understood the word. Appodiyos-- Ilokano for venerated god. It was a prayer. Under the circumstances, they could use help from any source they could get.

Samantha slumped against the wall. "So they created plants that can live off people. Why?"

"They didn't mean to. In making the plants able to hold larger crops, they gave them a muscular structure. In making them able to determine threats and annihilate them, they made them aggressive. What they could have avoided if they'd taken my research seriously is making the plants intelligent."

"Intelligent? That can't be possible."

"They've developed language, albeit more of a sign language, but they've also learned to transport information by forming minor manipulations on their genetics, like a genetically imprinted Morse code. From there, the minor genetic manipulations by humans turned to self-manipulations designed to help them reach their goal."

"Which is to kill everyone?"

"If necessary. Every creature's natural instinct is to grow and multiply. I'm sure they want out of here."

"Can we reason with them?"

Gerard shook his head. "If this had occurred naturally, then we probably could. But it appears they have no conscience. Only an animalistic need to proliferate."

"We need to destroy them, Gerard. We have to."

"It's too late for that." He reached down, pulling Miguel to his feet. "The crop torches are inside the facility and even if we could get to them, three of us wouldn't be enough to utilize them effectively. We have to tell someone what has happened."

Samantha nodded. "How do we get out?"

Gerard stared across the expanse of crops and overgrown vegetation to the gate. It had seemed like a fairly short walk on the way in. Now it resembled an impossible gauntlet.

"We'll get out the same way we came in," he said. "But a lot faster. The plants may be able to grow quickly and move their stalks and branches, but they're still stationary. We just have to get out before they can reach us. The most dangerous will be those petunias. Their thorns are wicked sharp and from what I gathered in the computer files, it appears they're the generals in the group."

"The flowers are in charge?"

Gerard nodded without humor. "Don't underestimate them."

Taking a deep breath, he opened the doors, shoving Samantha and Miguel ahead. "Run!"

They'd made it nearly halfway through the compound before the plants managed to anticipate them.

Samantha tripped. She caught herself, only a knee touching the dirt before rising up again.

"Keep going!" Gerard spoke through the two-way radio.

Miguel caught the swinging branch of a tomato plant in the shin. He plummeted forward, his torso landing among the furrows of plants and ripe, red fruit.

Gerard jumped Miguel's legs, avoiding the next swathe of the plant's thick branches. Only those closest to the path had grown to such lengths.

He glanced back. The tomato plants near the border were huge, even bigger than before. But those surrounding them had withered, fruit hanging heavily from limp stems, oozing into the hungry soil. In order to stop their prey, the plants had engaged in some combination of cannibalization and martyrdom, plants dying to give others the nutrients to grow faster.

Miguel screamed.

Samantha turned back.

Gerard waved her on. "Go! Get the gate open. I've got him."

Thick branches wrapped over Miguel's arm. They lacked the flexibility to encircle it, but dug again into the soil. A number of larger ones reached over his torso, as if trying to press him into the dirt. He convulsed, screaming. The branches stopped moving, holding him pinned as he jerked from side to side.

Gerard grabbed Miguel's legs. The strange seizure continued. It was as if a blender turned Miguel from the inside.

As Gerard dragged the man away, a squelching sound reverberated through his comm. link. It echoed distantly from outside Gerard's own suit. Blood smeared the dark earth. Gerard flipped him over. A gaping hole, oozing fluids, pierced the lower body.

Gerard continued to sidestep the tomato's grasping limbs as he worked pulled Miguel away. The limbs seemed to be moving slower, groggier for some reason. Perhaps its sudden growth had used up its lifespan.

"I'm so sorry," Gerard told Miguel, prepared to run on.

"Please...help me. Don't...don't leave me...not here." Miguel gasped between lips dripping red spittle.

Gerard stared. How could the man still be alive? Did he dare bring him? But Gerard couldn't leave him out here. It was too inhumane.

Hoisting the small man into a fireman's carry, he took off again. No doubt, Miguel's blood ran down the back of his yellow suit. Not that it mattered. Gerard doubted he'd survive to the gate.

The plants continued to block his path, but Gerard clumsily stepped out of their way. Not much farther now.

He reached the detox chamber to find thick flower tendrils encasing the boxy structure. Only a small space in front of the door, just enough space for a single body, remained free. Those doors were open, jammed at the halfway point, crushing the plant-life wedged inside the door mechanism.

Samantha waited on the other side, beckoning Gerard to hurry. Like a sack of potatoes, he hoisted Miguel off his back. Gerard tossed him through the narrow opening as the sky rained black pellets—the petunia seeds. They bounced across his back. Pattering like hail, they pelted the metal door and bounced inside the chamber with Miguel and Samantha.

Gerard threw himself after Miguel, sliding on the man's gore. Petunia pods burst around the outside of the chamber, one right after the other. By the time Gerard's momentum stopped, he lay on his back pressing the Filipino's body into the opposite door, surrounded by black seeds. .

Samantha managed to seal the doors, slicing off a green shoot with the closing panels. It fell onto the floor, oozing sap.

"Quick!" Gerard snapped. "Hit the detox button.

Before any of these seeds can take root."

Samantha slammed her hand across the red button.

Gerard came to his feet again, nearly slipping on the wet, textured metal. In the center of the chamber a miniscule whirlpool drained the ichorous fluids filling the space. Not enough to be effective. He turned Miguel over, hoping to cleanse his wound in the herbicidal spray. The shower suddenly stopped, dripping from the walls and ceiling like thick urine.

Miguel stared up at Gerard, unblinking. A wilted yellowish seedling, about the size of Gerard's pinkie finger, extended through the hole in his suit.

Gerard nearly vomited. Hands on his knees, he took deep breaths. He needed to calm down, but the stifling suit only added to his anxiety. When the room stopped spinning and his vision cleared, he recognized Samantha's panicked voice as the ringing in his ears.

"Why did it stop, Gerard? What do we do?"

"The plants," he said, leaning his shoulders against one seeping wall. "They must have found a way into the delivery system or the computer.

She clutched his arm. "Then they'll be in here next."

Gerard shook his head. "The delivery system computer is in the building with the mainframe. The pipes with the herbicide run from there to the detox chambers."

"But if they're in the pipes--"

"Then they're dead. Clogging up the pipes. Eventually, live ones will break through, but it will take days or weeks, even for these mutants."

Samantha visibly relaxed. For a moment, Gerard thought she might faint, go into shock. She leaned her hand against the wall next to Gerard's face, taking deep breaths. "Now what?"

"We wait for the room to drain, get out of our suits, and get to civilization as fast as we possibly can."

Samantha nodded. "The company needs to know about this immediately."

Gerard snorted. "Yeah, BFA needs to know about it. So does the CDC, the USDA, the FBI, probably some acronyms I've never heard of and don't want to know about, and the leadership and military of at least both countries."

"The BFA won't like the idea of letting this out."

"Have I ever cared about what the BFA wants? They've just created the most dangerous enemy the human race will probably ever face. If it's not controlled within days...days, not weeks or months... we'll be in a full scale war I'm not sure we can win."

A slurping noise erupted from the drain at their feet. The last of the fluid finally drained, leaving behind the heavier petunia seeds. They sat trapped between the raised patterns in the metal floor, resting in shallow pools of ichor.

Gerard fumbled with the sealed zipper running up the length of the hazmat suit. With three layers of gloves it was a little tricky.

Samantha put a hand to his arm. "Wait. Won't we be safer with the suits on?"

"Yes, but the rest of the world won't be. If even one of those seeds is stuck in the groove of a helmet, a textured boot, or a fold of plastic we could be putting every human on this planet in danger. We'll stay right by the exit. Very carefully, top to bottom, one complete layer at a time, take the suit off and place the pieces behind you. Boots and latex gloves go last."

Samantha nodded, fumbling at her own zipper. Her shaking fingers couldn't manage it. When Gerard reached his second layer, he stopped to help. She peeled the bright orange jumpsuit away, pulled off her breathing apparatus, cooling vest, and outer silver protective gloves. Turning to place them behind her, she cried out. Her hands slapped at the middle of her back, reaching for something, her eyes wide.

Gerard dropped the Tyvek jumpsuit layer to the ankles of his hiking boots. "What's wrong? I don't see anything. What--"

"The petunia thorns. One ripped through!" Samantha screamed. "The suits are supposed to be impermeable. How could...how could...." She dropped her hands, staring up at him with tears streaming down her cheeks. "You'll have to leave me. We can't risk one of these things making it outside the barriers."

Gerard stared at her pale features; thick dark hair matted against her face. Restrained terror shone bright in her tear-stained eyes. He loved her. They'd never even been on a date, but they'd eaten lunch together, bantered in the office, and talked science with each other for nearly a year. He'd rather die than leave her behind.

But would he be willing to risk killing the people in this country, maybe the world, by letting those monsters find their way out?

"Let me see," he said with a calm he didn't feel.

Samantha pointed to the orange jumpsuit lying across the blood-stained floor next to her gear. A wide gash ran the length of one side. Gerard couldn't tell where it placed on Samantha's body.

"You didn't feel anything?"

Samantha whimpered, but shook her head.

Gerard turned her back to face him. Another gash, identical to the one in the encapsulation suit, ran the length of the Tyvek layer; from the top of her shoulder blades to the curve of her buttocks. He clenched the edges of the material and pulled it aside. His gloved hands reached in and settled on the fabric around her slim waist. He touched his forehead to her shoulder, and let out a heavy breath.

"It didn't go through your clothes. You're okay."

Gerard released his hold. The peeled layers of her suit rustled as she turned to face him.

"Are you sure? None of us put on the jumpsuits we're supposed to have on under the Tyvek. We can't--"

"I'm positive. And I'm not leaving you behind."

He almost touched her face, but remembering his latex-gloved fingers, he stopped.

Tears running down her cheeks, she wrapped her arms around him, nestling against his shoulder. He held her tight until she calmed.

He would have liked to remain that way, holding her forever rather than deal with what lay ahead. Gently, he grasped her shoulders and pushed her back.

He pulled down the front zipper of her paper-like Tyvek suit. "Let's get out of here."

After some struggles with her outer firefighting boots, they stepped through the decontamination chamber door into the next perimeter of barren wasteland. Each of them peeled off their gloves, throwing them in with the dismantled hazmat-wear, and then sealed the door behind them.

Standing in the blackened soil, they exhaled their

relief. Gerard pulled Samantha into a real embrace, no suits or gloves between them. He wrapped his arms around her as if she might disappear.

Glancing across the expanse of barren dirt, she pulled away. "We have to hur--"

Gerard grabbed her elbow, pulling her back. He kissed her, letting all the fear, frustration, and final relief of the last few hours blend with the kiss. She hesitated at first, but to his grateful surprise, she met his intensity, twining her fingers in his hair.

They eventually pulled apart, and Gerard took her hand. "Timing probably wasn't the best for this," Gerard admitted. "But I don't know what will happen when we reach civilization, or what will happen with those crazy mutant plants. I didn't want to wait another second without letting you know how I feel."

Samantha smiled. "I'd been hoping you'd eventually make some kind of move. I thought dinner or drinks would come first, but this works."

"I can be a little dense."

"That's an understatement." They clasped hands, and started across the barren landscape.

Even with a clear path, it took a few hours to make their way back. Miguel's beat-up truck waited uselessly for them. They hadn't thought to grab the keys and neither of them knew how to hot-wire a car. The sun was dipping toward the horizon as they walked the narrow winding road making switchbacks up to the mountain toward Baguio City. But luck hadn't completely deserted them.

A jeepney--the Filipinos' garish version of a WWII troop transport jeep retrofitted for public transportation--sluggishly made its way up the road.

Gerard hailed it down.

The driver shook his head, gesturing to the filled seats behind him and the two men hanging off the back. He jabbered something in his own language. The sing-song of his voice as he spoke the repetitive syllables of his language brought Miguel's dead body to mind. He pushed the image away, reaching into his back pocket.

Holding up two fifty-peso bills, he extended them to the driver. The garish reddish-orange of the money almost matched the red flames competing with a circus of other colors and designs splashed across the bright yellow jeepney. For Gerard, the pesos didn't mean much more than ten or twenty bucks--a t-shirt. For this man, it might mean a new roof or food for a month.

The bright bills caught the man's attention. "Nasaan ka pupunta?"

Gerard shook his head. "I don't understand. I no speak...um...Ilokano?"

The men with him in the cab laughed.

"Where you go?" asked the driver.

"Baguio," said Gerard.

"Any city," added Samantha.

Gerard nodded.

The man shrugged. "Baguio. You hold on."

As the driver yelled to the two men hanging off the back, Gerard and Samantha shook the collected mud off their shoes, scraping them against the edges of the worn, cracked asphalt.

The two men in the back piled into the cab with the men already there. It was like something from a clown show. Gerard and Samantha took their place, clinging to the back of the truck. A young man sitting at the end ushered Samantha to take his seat, swinging to the back next to Gerard. Since arriving in their country, Gerard had never seen a woman or older person hanging off the side of a jeepney or any of their other makeshift vehicles. The younger men always made space for them; a rare gesture in America anymore.

"What are we going to do, Gerard?" Samantha said before the jeepney started up again. "About the plants."

Gerard's eyes hardened. "We're going to spray, burn, and destroy every plant, root and seed in that compound."

"But I thought you believed--"

"Having monstrosities like those threaten people you care about can change a man's perspective. Besides, those plants are nothing like natural evolution would have created."

As they pulled away, the sputtering engine coming to life, Samantha grabbed a fistful of Gerard's shirt. She screamed something, pointing behind them. Over the grinding of the gears and the blaring of the driver's sound system, he couldn't make out the words.

He glanced over his shoulder and nearly lost his grip. He gaped at the remains of dirt and mud clinging to his and Samantha's boots. What had they done? Jaw slack, he returned his gaze to where they'd stood by the road only a few moments ago.

Coming into bloom, surrounded by dead and dying plants, was an enormous petunia. Its violet petals, streaked with veins like blood, opened toward a fluorescent Filipino sunset.

Author's Note:

My daughter was the impetus for this story. We'd been at a church function where she'd received baskets with these giant paper flowers attached, and we started joking about wearing it to school and one-upping all the girls who were into the current trend of wearing flowers in their hair. From there, the conversation degenerated.

By the time we finished, we'd decided that the flowers on girls' heads looked like vegetation had taken root in their brains and started growing like monsters taking over the world. That's how I remember the conversation, anyway.

My daughter used the idea in a short story for a class assignment and I went on to write *Eden's Hell*. It's one of the funnest projects I've ever put together. No one who read these stories has looked at either one of us quite the same ever since.

Obsessions

Another beautiful morning in Southern Utah; bees, birds, and other wildlife noised around the Blue Mountain forests and meadows as if nothing unexpected had ever happened. The greenery, in early-summer bloom, rustled from a soft breeze. Wildflowers dotted the landscape, their faint perfume mixing with the smell of Pine and Quaking Aspen. We'd already seen a few deer and elk as we hiked nearer the mountain's "horse head"—a large space devoid of trees, facing the nearby town of Monticello. Reminiscent of the days when nature had sculpted the head of a horse by its random dispersal of plant life, the faint outline could still be seen if one gazed long enough. Nothing felt out of place. None of the wildlife seemed jumpy or easily startled. Even the fresh scat that stuck to my heavy hiking boots as I wandered off trail, smelled as bad as any other day.

Ferrin flipped a quaker branch in my face.

I jerked my hand up—too slow. It smacked me

square on the nose. "Blast! Would you stop it already? We're not cub scouts."

Ferrin's laughter rumbled ahead of me.

Pushing the branch aside, I stepped back on the trail. "Hey, you ever heard my great-grandfather's story about how Blue Mountain got its name?"

"It's because the greenery is so rich it seems blue." Ferrin responded.

"Not according to Steer Chamberlain," Gareth yelled from somewhere up ahead. "Aliens! But Steer was nuts. He spent every waking moment with his cattle—breeding them, feeding them, petting them...The guy had a screw loose. Maybe that's where Drex gets it from--inherited."

I forced a laugh. "If I'm crazy, you're psychotic. The story is family legend now. We laugh about it at reunions, and sometimes--." I stopped, staring at a glob of coagulated blue Jello amid a stretch of yellowed grass. It stunk of overripe fruit. "What—?"

Ferrin snapped another branch at my face. Trying to avoid it, I stumbled. My foot slipped in the puddle of goop, and I went down. My back landed on something hard, a bit bigger than a softball. But that wasn't what made me cry out. My hand slipped into another puddle of blue snot, searing pain spreading across my fingers. Screaming, I sat up, shaking the vile goop away. Spit-wad size pellets scattered in every direction.

"Ow! Stop that!" Ferrin wiped a spot off his cheek.

I grabbed my water bottle from my pack, pouring the cool liquid over my hand. The blue gel washed off as easily as finger-paint, leaving my hand a bright red with a number of small blisters.

The miniscule blob that hit Ferrin left a red mark

and a pit like a blackhead crater. Since it was Ferrin, nobody would notice the new addition. Ferrin was helping me fish some salve from my backpack when Gareth finally backtracked to see what was taking us so long.

"What happened?" he asked.

"Don't touch the attack Jello!" I yelled.

I reached for the salve Ferrin had smeared on his cheek. "I told you Jello casseroles are evil." I smeared the burn cream over my finger, gently rubbing it in. "Now I have proof."

Ferrin helped me with the salve and wrapped my hand in a roll of first-aid gauze. "Sure, the stuff is dangerous when you put carrot shavings and raisins in it, but it's not supposed to eat off your skin during a mountain hike."

Ferrin's jeans had turned soot black and threadbare where he'd wiped his hands. I looked to my boots. The blue gel dripped from the rubber with no distinguishable effect. I shifted away from the "rock" I'd landed on, finding something less expected than the caustic Jello. A strange metallic sphere glinted in the sunlight streaming between the branches.

"Blimey, what is that?"

Gareth stepped from between a couple of trees, careful of the blue splotch. "You've been back from England for a whole year, Drex. When are you going to lose the British crap?"

"Why should I?" I laughed, picking up a sharp stick. "All the girls think it's hot."

Ferrin laughed. "He's got you there. Every girl in Monticello, Blanding, and probably all of southeastern Utah wants a date with him before he heads back to college."

"Considering the population of southeastern Utah, that's what, three girls?" said Gareth in obvious exaggeration. "And two of them look like my Aunt Lettie's horse."

"Forget it," I said. "Come take a look at this thing."

Ferrin squatted to get a better view.

Gareth sighed, making his way around Ferrin. "What's the point of even dating out here? I'm a Redd, Ferrin is a Black and Drex is a Chamberlain. Everyone in both towns is related to us at least once. We'd end up with kids that have six toes or—." He squatted closer, finally able to see the orb. "What the--?"

"Hey, you just returned from a church mission, remember?" Ferrin reminded him. "None of that."

"I was going to say heck."

"I'm sure you were," I said, not hiding my sarcasm. Gareth had been thrown out of more than a few church basketball games on account of his language.

I poked it with the stick. "I landed on it when I slipped in the attack-Jello." Hunching over, I took a closer look. The casing appeared to be Navajo silver and melted turquoise swirled together, the individual strands of color mixing into one bluish hue. "Hold on, I think there's writing on it."

Ferrin snatched it up. "Do you think it could be Egyptian?"

"On a mountain in Utah? Sure, and Arches National Park is full of pyramids."

There was an expulsion of air. Ferrin jerked his head back, blinking. A stream of blood ran from his left tear duct along the side of his large nose.

I placed a hand on his shoulder, trying to inspect his rapidly blinking eye. "Whoa! Ferrin, you all right?"

He shook his head, still blinking. The stream slowed

to a couple of drops then stopped. He pulled a tissue from his pocket, wiping them away. "I'm fine. The inscriptions are amazing. Take a look."

"Are you barmy? Your brain is freaking bleeding. I don't think—" He pressed the ball into my hands. It tingled, unnaturally warm. The black circular inscriptions drew me closer. Air blew into my eye, like a pin had entered through my pupil to the back of my eye-socket. The pain only lasted a fraction of a second, replaced by pure ecstasy. I blinked and tears formed. The next instant, I remembered nothing but the pleasant puff and that the inscription was amazing. Gareth had to hold the ball. He had to see…whatever I'd seen.

I smiled down at him, reaching out with the orb. "Here. The inscriptions are brilliant. Take a look."

Gareth backed away. "Uh, you guys are doing the zombie act pretty well on your own. I'll just get going." He took a tentative step back.

Ferrin stared into space, unconcerned. I followed Gareth. I wanted to stop, to leave him alone, but I had to give Gareth that ball more than I'd had to kiss Tracy Dunnin at my senior prom. It *had* to happen.

Gareth turned and ran, but he only made a few steps before I tackled him down. I pressed the orb to his cheek, sickened at my exultant success. His eyes glazed. He rolled onto his back, gripping the ball. At that point, I no longer cared. I released him and joined Ferrin, staring into space.

After a few minutes, Ferrin shoved me. "I've got studying to do. We need to get back."

I nodded, the trees coming back into focus. Ferrin didn't have any summer classes. He shouldn't need to study, but I didn't really care. I had more important things to worry about.

I blinked, shook my head, and realized I'd wasted my entire weekend camping on that mountain. "You're right. We' have to get out of here." Gareth still held the ball, staring into space. I tried pulling him to his feet, but he didn't respond.

"Leave him," said Ferrin.

"Friends take priority over schedules," I said in a monotone. I'd seen enough zombie movies that that should have frightened me. "Help me."

Ferrin threw Gareth over his back. "Anything to get me home sooner. I have important studies, you know."

We dragged Gareth through the woods. After a few minutes, he shook us off. "I've got to get home. Now."

We gathered our gear, drove down Blue Mountain, past the high school, and into Monticello. At the edge of town, Margenine Butler walked down the the street with her kids. Her two oldest, Moroni and Sariah, held each side of a double stroller. The two youngest, Nephi and Geminah sat inside. Lucky for Geminah, her parents had run out of Mormon-based names they'd liked. Unlucky for her, they'd started searching their family history.

Gareth's face perked up and his eyes regained their focus. "Let me out."

"What?" I said. "We're three blocks from your house."

"Let me out now!" Gareth screamed, reaching for the door handle, scrambling over Ferrin.

"Dude!" said Ferrin. "We're not that good of friends."

I pulled over as Gareth tumbled from the truck, the orb clenched in his sweaty hand. He ran to the sidewalk, pressing the ball to Margenine Butler's pregnant belly. She released the stroller to clasp the ball.

It bothered me, but I couldn't think why, couldn't say anything. Gareth jumped back in, and I pulled away. Glancing in my rear-view mirror I saw Margenine with a line of red down her face. She handed the orb to Sariah. I shivered, revolted, but drove on.

A San Juan county phone book rested between the front seats, almost as big as the pamphlet sitting on top of it. Gareth snatched it up. His finger ran down the names on the front page. Grabbing a pen, he started circling numbers.

"Hey," I reached for the booklet. "I might need that."

Gareth clamped it close to his chest. The feral look in his eye convinced me to let it go.

We reached Ferrin's house. He jumped out of the truck as soon as I'd slowed down, before I could put it in park. "Hey," I yelled after him, "what about your gear?"

"Throw it on the lawn."

Gareth had me do the same with his camping equipment, frantically pressing numbers on his cell phone, ecstatic he'd reached three bars of signal.

I shook my head. "You guys really should take better care of your stuff."

As Gareth stepped from the truck, he spoke into the phone. "Carol, you're not related to me in any way, right? Would you like to go to the movies with me? Right now....I guess I can wait until tonight...."

I was too focused on myself to worry about Ferrin and Gareth. When I reached home, I pulled out my phone, accessing the Franklin Planner app I'd bought six months ago and never opened, filling out my priority list—church studies, family time, service, friends…. It took three hours to set everything in order. Nothing outside of my schedule entered my mind for the next week.

The summer heat hadn't reached unbearable, making the park clear and green for the church picnic. I'd heard there was new blood in town, and dating had a place in my priorities. As soon as I parked the truck, I spotted her, not a difficult accomplishment in a small town.

Chantelle stood near the grill, hooking dark hair behind perfect ears, letting it waterfall down her back. She beamed the epitome of perfect mate.

Like always, Bertol Perkins—the church barbeque guru--stood at the grill flipping mounds of seasoned meat. Within a couple of minutes I'd managed to get myself next to Chantelle, paper plate in hand. Behind us, the line started to back up.

"Brother Perkins, the line's getting a bit long," I said good-naturedly. "I'll take a medium-rare if you've got one."

His fat face, flushed from the heat of the grill, sneered. "The perfect hamburger takes time, you little twit. You'll wait until it's ready. That goes for the rest of you yahoos, too!" He narrowed his eyes, scaring the children into hiding behind their parents' legs.

Before I could respond Sister Bernadette Shumway shoved a spoonful of lime Jello into my mouth. "You'll love this."

I tried not to gag. Not that gelatin desserts are bad, but there's something about the texture. I've never been able to get over the similarity to those gag gifts in a can, the ones that fart when you squish them around. I held it in my mouth, took a deep breath through my nose, and swallowed, tears filling my eyes

Her face fell. "It's still not perfect!"

"Sister Shumway, blimey, it's all right. It's me, not the Jello."

"No." Her feverish eyes forced me back a step. "When I get it right, everyone will love it. I need more Jello." She wiped a bead of sweat from her brow. "The Blanding stores are out. I'll have to drive to Farmington." She continued to talk to herself as she ran for the parking lot.

"This has to be the strangest place in existence," Chantelle muttered next to me.

"That does seem a bit odd." I said, but couldn't quite focus on why.

"A bit?" She turned on me, an attractive fire to her eyes. "Anyone who is leaving a party so they can drive four hours to buy Jello is nuts." She brought her voice to a whisper. "Everyone I've met in this place is bonkers."

"Wait a minute, how do you mean?" Even as I asked the question, I could feel my brain pressing against some invisible barrier. Priorities, this had something to do with priorities. I could focus on that.

"Some guy, Gareth Redd, is walking around asking girls to marry him. He even asked me, and he didn't know my name yet. I met a woman who hasn't stopped reading her bible for two days, not even to eat. My aunt's neighbor hasn't stopped working on his yard for two days. He had halogen spotlights shining around his yard at three o'clock this morning so he could trim the hedges one twig at a time." She rubbed her eyes and yawned. "I'm still seeing spots. When we left this afternoon, he was hand-trimming his grass. That's insane. I mean, that's beyond a priority imbalance."

The pressure in my mind grew. "You're right. I'm glad my priorities aren't so messed up. I put first things first."

"But nobody seems to care either. Every time I think someone else sees the weirdness, they get distracted. They end up being as weird as everyone else. The whole county seems focused on that ridiculous ball."

Chantelle gestured to the silver-blue orb. I hadn't noticed it. Sister Johnson, a red streak down her cheek, handed the ball to my sister. I lurched forward, thinking to stop her, then couldn't.

I blinked. "What were we saying?"

"See." She threw up one hand, the other still waiting for the perfect hamburger. "You claim you have your priorities in order, but you're as crazy as the rest of them."

I dropped my plate, pressing my palms to my pounding head. Light flared inside my skull. I had to ignore the ball, but if priorities mattered then I couldn't. The ideas warred, the pain increased. I groaned. Light and agony pierced my head in one last torturous blast. I dropped to my knees and the world went black.

I woke to find Chantelle kneeling at my side. Her soft hands touched the rough stubble of one cheek. "Are you all right? What happened?"

She smelled of fresh gardenias. "I'm...I don't know,

but I have one heck of a headache."

She helped me to my feet. I swayed for a moment, but she held onto me and I considered ways to tell her how amazingly gorgeous she was, but I had other priorities at the moment.

Blood dripping from one eye, Clary pressed the ball into Crydin Pugh's hands.

I grabbed the orb. "No! This has to stop."

The pain in my head pulsed. Crydin wrenched the ball from my loose fingers, placing the inscriptions to his eye.

My mom claimed caffeine helped with her migraines. I grabbed the 2-liter of Dr. Pepper Brother Perkins was using for his marinade and chugged it down. It didn't really help, but I felt less dehydrated.

Sister Redd yanked the bottle from my mouth as I licked at the last drops. "Drinking caffeine is a sin, young man. Repent, I say unto you, repent." She shook a finger between my eyes.

This was my crazy Grandpa Chamberlain's obsession all over again, only the entire town was getting infected. He'd been a devoted cattle rancher until he'd flipped and started spending every waking moment with the cattle. Come to think of it, he slept with them, too. Now everyone in town was finding something in their lives to obsess over.

Crydin shoved the ball at Chantelle. "See the Orb," he said like a bad horror flick. I might have laughed if he wasn't about to make my girlfriend-to-be into a similar glazy-eyed crazy person. I toyed with the thought that her orb-induced excess might include a need to get personal with the handsomest guy closest to her, but then realized the chances of that were pretty slim.

As her fingertips made contact, I pulled the orb from her grasp. Who knew, she might start shoving Jello in my face if I let her keep hold.

"Hey," she and Crydin said together.

I tucked the orb tight to my side. "You do *not* want to touch this ball."

"I *do* want to touch it." She blinked, shook her head. "But I think you're right. I'd better not."

"Just think of it as a Jehovah's Witness going door-to-door with pamphlets. That should curb the impulse."

Crydin desperately grabbed for it, but I kept a firm hold. "Clear off, kid. For your own good." I grabbed Chantelle's hand. "Come on."

We ran for my truck, Crydin giving chase, the fervor in his eyes surpassing anything I'd seen from the young man in church.

Though in pretty good condition at the ripe old age of twenty-three, I couldn't compete with a sixteen-year-old track star. Crydin's scrawny frame tackled me to the asphalt. My arm cleared the parking lot of debris. My face served as the brake.

From the corner of my eye, I watched Chantelle do a roundhouse to Crydin's face. She front-kicked his chest and he skidded across the asphalt on his back. Lucky for him, I'd already cleaned that section.

I sat up. "I'll be gobsmacked."

"I heard you like to impress the ladies with your Brit crap. My pappy's from Yorkshire, so don't bother."

"I don't do it on purpose." It was almost the truth. "It's just me."

She tore the keys from my hands. "Jump in. I'll drive while you take care of the blood all over your face."

Chantelle peeled out from the parking lot, something I didn't know my old Chevy pickup could do. Crydin ran behind us for three country blocks before he tripped and gave up.

Grabbing an old t-shirt from the old Chevy's floorboard, I pressed it to my bleeding head. "Did you study under Jackie Chan, or maybe Charlie's Angels?"

Chantelle laughed. It was a beautiful laugh. "I studied Tae Kwon Do. Made second degree black belt before I decided I didn't have time for it anymore. Now what is going on? What is that ball and why do I still feel like I need to hold it. If you hadn't taken it away, I'm not sure what would have happened, but I know it wouldn't have been good. And who are you?"

I reached out a hand. "Drexel Chamberlain." I didn't blame her for not taking it, not once I realized it was smeared with blood. I tucked my hand back into the sweat-encrusted t-shirt. I had to be making a great impression here. "I'm the one who found this thing. Whatever's going on, it's my fault."

Chantelle shook her head. "Nobody cared that you fell into that seizure. Nobody cared that two adults were having it out with a teenage boy in a parking lot. Half the people in the park had blood seeping from their eyes. What is that thing?"

"Not half," said my scientific self. "More like a third."

Her stare told me I was not doing well on the girlfriend-to-be path. I decided the numbers weren't such a priority.

"It does something, magic or science I don't know, but I suspect science. When I held it the first time, my hands became really warm. I think it secreted a chemical into my bloodstream, something neurological. It squirts something through the pupil that travels to the brain. I knew something was going on, but I couldn't think about it, not until you kept telling me my priorities were out of whack. Something broke loose, and now I can think about it. I can disregard my compulsion to ignore the ball, and I'm aware that I'm obsessing over priorities."

"So what can we do?"

I frowned, concentrating. "After Ferrin and Gareth touched the orb, Ferrin became obsessed with the need to go study because he's been worried about his Spring semester grades. Gareth started calling the first girl he could think of because he's been focused on dating and finding a wife. Brother Chamberlain has always prided himself on his role as barbeque master, and Sis. Shumway always had a penchant for Jello. This orb plays on whatever is important to us, making us focus on one important aspect of our lives to the exclusion of all else. But why? What's the point?"

"What were you focused on?"

"Turn here. Third house on the right." I shook my head. "Getting my priorities in order. I had a Franklin Planner, though I didn't get consistent using it until a week ago—the day I touched the orb. And I bought about five more planning apps that day."

"So when I pushed you into thinking about the people affected as the first priority…."

I nodded. "…it contradicted the programming in my brain. You made it so I could finally act."

Chantelle pulled into my driveway. My family hadn't come home yet, but they'd all been infected at the party. They'd probably be home soon. I clenched a fist. I'd come to my senses too late.

Chantelle opened her truck door. "So, if we can find

103

a way to contradict the person's obsession related to the existence of the orb, we can undo everything?"

I found my keys and joined her at the front door. "Maybe, but I have a feeling some will be easier to convince than others. We need more information."

"At your house?"

"My grandfather has an interesting journal."

She shrugged. "Where's your first aid kit? We need to get you cleaned up."

I directed her to a medicine cabinet in the bathroom, as I went to the basement. On my father's dusty bookshelf I found the spiral-bound life history of Sterling "Steer" Chamberlain.

Chantelle waited for me at the kitchen table; bandages, cleaners, and other tools of torture spread before her. She cleaned and treated my wounds, oblivious to my grimaces of pain, then inspected her work with a soft touch. I gazed into her large blue-green eyes. They drew me forward. I'd only known Chantelle for about two hours, but she didn't move away.

The front lock unlatched. We jumped away from each other. Thank the family for excellent timing—not. Swiping the first-aid debris from the table to the kitchen garbage, I put everything in order as Chantelle put the containers back in the medicine cabinet. We made a good team, slipping out the back door before my mother reached the kitchen.

"Oh, this place is a mess!" They were words I'd heard before, but never with such vehemence. Besides, we'd cleaned house that morning. "I haven't washed the windows for over a week. I need to clean the baseboards and those curtains haven't been laundered since last month. I bet there are dust bunnies under the bed too."

The orb. She'd become obsessed with a clean house.

We snuck round the side to the truck. While I scanned my grandfather's journal, Chantelle drove us to the home of the craziest man in town--ex-marine, Creg MacPhearson.

The Aliens of Blue Mountain, I read from the journal, *As I remember from my da's stories:*

Supposedly, da and some buddies were hiking around Blue Mountain. A ship the size of ten barns, looking like Navajo jewelry, landed in a meadow. Creatures like giant raindrops rolled down a long ramp to the ground. These balloon-men took him in a container and done experiments on him. He said his friend, Jake, was ate by one of them. Nobody believed it. Jake had been wanting to skip town most his life. Later, my da changed the story, said Jake done run away, but he still told us kids it was the blue monsters.

He'd always say he could have killed them easy if they hadn't done some mind trick on him while searching for his "human weakness." If they looked for vices in da, I'm sure they found some mighty fine ones. He was a wild one in his early years. He did a bit of cattle rustling and such, and he was known to take the occasional drink even afore this all happened and he started spending all his time with his herd and his whiskey. It's one hell of a dream or a nightmare, though."

I studied Chantelle from the corner of my eye. "Do you think...?"

"I think it's utterly ridiculous. But that stupid ball is still staring at me, telling me to touch it."

We pulled in front of MacPhearson's house and I set

the journal on the dashboard. "I think we need to get help."

"Everyone is infected," said Chantelle. "Besides, what are you going to tell people?"

I gripped Chantelle's shoulder, looking her in the eye. "I'm going to lie through my teeth. We need people and we need firearms. We saw a huge mountain lion up on the Blue." I pointed out my scrapes and bruises. "I lost my gun to the beast and barely made it out alive."

Chantelle smiled. "This is kind of fun."

Oh yeah, truly in love. I leaned forward. Chantelle pressed a hand against my chest, holding me back. "I've only known you a few hours."

I raised an eyebrow. "My dad only knew my mom a few days before he proposed. It's a family thing."

Black-belts make great kissers.

It took some convincing, but within a few hours we rolled up the road onto Blue Mountain in a large convoy. A few orb-affected people even joined in, compelled by the orb to focus on the need to hunt, protect their families, or live off the land. We convinced one guy with an Armageddon stash of firearms in his basement that the government created the mutant lion to slow population growth. I told Gareth it would make him look brave to the ladies, and Ferrin that it was a study in animal behavior which would help his advanced biology class come Fall.

I drove my truck, guiding everyone toward the horse head. "Do you think they did the same thing all over the world at once?"

"It's possible, Chantelle said, "but I doubt it. I talked to my family in San Diego last night. Everything seems absolutely normal there. I think we're a test region."

Leaving the trucks, I strapped an Uzi to my back, grabbed the orb, and a sledgehammer. As we neared the horse-head meadow. I spotted the ship--round, bright blue, and enormous. I ran ahead, stopping when I'd come within a few feet. The line of men moved forward, open-mouthed, though Gareth and Ferrin stayed at the back staring in fear.

A few men ran, but the rest gathered close. A tall rectangular seam disrupted the smooth ship's surface. The rectangle detached, forming a ramp.

"Keep back," I yelled. "These things might be dangerous."

"This ain't no mountain lion!" MacPhearson yelled.

"Sorry, bloke. Would you have believed me if I'd said man-eating aliens? So, we're not defending the local community from a measly mountain lion. We might be defending the world from an invading force of Jello gone wrong. You man enough?"

MacPhearson and the men clenched their weapons, faces determined. We were ready—as ready as we could be.

From inside the spaceship, a bright blue blob appeared. It reminded me of berry gelatin shapes my nephews had made and played with as they gobbled off their heads. The creature's eyes, the same bright color as its gelatinous body, glistened in the sunlight. Stubby appendages poked from its side like blue Mr. Potato arms. It tucked them in, rolling down the plank like a half-full water balloon.

At the end of the runway, it stopped, sloshing from

side to side. With careful precision, it rolled onto the uneven ground, beaming with child-like triumph, exhibiting a toothless smile. It beckoned us forward, innocent as a young child.

Terry Dalton stepped from the group. "We don't have to kill it. This is a chance at first contact." He extended his hands in a sign of surrender, moving closer to the alien.

"No, Terry," I said. "Step back!"

The slim plastic-like hand shook Terry's, its smile still wide and unassuming. It grabbed his elbow. Using Terry as an anchor, it slid belly to belly with him.

"Wait." Terry tried to step back.

The alien jiggled, a Smurf-version Santa Clause, pulling Terry's arm into its blue belly. He screamed. Steam rose. The gelatinous blob opened its shallow mouth in delighted pleasure. It grabbed the sides of Terry's shirt, enveloping him, the wails coming to a sudden stop.

I went for my Uzi.

The monster smiled, like a child hoping for another lollipop. I hated flavored gelatin with a new fervor.

It beckoned again. We stepped away.

The blob rolled forward. Someone finally came to their senses and fired.

Like an overfilled water balloon, it burst.

"Take cover!" I yelled.

Gelatinous goop, smelling of rotten fruit, spattered through the air. Chantelle and I dove behind a wide pine at the edge of the meadow.

A few trees away, MacPhearson yelled over. "So what are we fighting here?"

"It's Jello gone bad, MacPhearson. Every church-going man's worst nightmare."

108

Blue creatures poured from the ship. They had to slow down when they reached the dirt, presumably to avoid sharp objects. Half our force screamed and ran down the hill.

"Wait!" I yelled after them. "We have to stop them!"

"This ain't no mountain lion, Drex!" one of the men called as he ran. "We need the National Guard!"

There were maybe a dozen of us left.

"If we don't stop them here, we'll never stop them!" I stared MacPhearson in the eye.

He nodded. "They're not getting past us," he said loud enough to bolster the rest of the men.

I nodded back. Hefting my sledgehammer, I walked to the edge of the trees. I placed the orb on the ground within sight of the aliens. I raised the sledgehammer. Swung it down. The orb fell apart, crumbling into tiny bits. A small sphere of blue goo slipped from its core. Ugh, did the stuff have to be everywhere? In my head, the barrier dimmed. I still felt compelled, but it became a small nudge, easily ignored. I saw a similar effect on Ferrin and Gareth, who'd been standing in the background. With the orb's destruction, they shook their heads, flipped the safety off their rifles, and took cover behind a pair of boulders, revenge in their eyes.

As the ooze slipped from the orb to the dirt, one of the aliens popped, its Jello-like parts flying over its comrades. They absorbed the bits and pieces, unbothered.

They turned toward me, jiggling. Laughing?

As one, each alien reached into its belly and pulled out an identical orb. One of them, wearing a device akin to black ear muffs--some kind of translator-- spoke. The alien jiggled, and a computer-generated voice sounded from the muffs. "You cannot resist us. We have studied your kind and you are ruled by your obsessions." He grabbed another alien's orb and rolled it toward me. "Touch the ball and see the future."

I hammered the thing. "See your future, you freaking lump of gush!"

I ducked behind the tree as the alien popped.

They'd judged the entire human race on their study of my ancestor. They'd chosen a poor specimen and I intended to prove their error.

I ran back out into the open. It was time to spill some Jello. "Take cover!"

I opened fire. Each bullet passed through four or five of them before it stopped. Blue beads of acid flew high into the air. I wouldn't make it back to the tree and even if I could, it wasn't wide enough to protect myself and Chantelle together. I curled up, waiting for the pain. Everything turned blue, but I didn't feel anything. Chantelle squatted next to me, a blue tarp covering us both, goop splattering it in large plops. It fizzled, but as with my shoe when I'd first discovered the orb, plastic was resilient.

"Where--?" I asked.

"MacPhearson had a tarp in his pack." Chantelle pulled at my arm. "I think you motivated the other men." Bullets continued to fire and goop continued to rain. "Now, let's get behind some trees. The tarp can only take so much."

We waddled to safety, and Chantelle stuck a finger to my face. "You could have been killed."

I shrugged. "There wasn't room behind that tree to keep us both safe."

She shook her head in the universal sign meaning stupid men. But then she kissed me. Stupidity can have some advantages.

Each of us now behind a tree, I scanned the area. The men were attacking in rounds. Everyone shot, and then everyone ducked while the goo splattered. Most of the men only had 22's or, at best, a shotgun. Some of the monsters ran for the ship, popping randomly if they went too fast over a stick or sharp rock, but some advanced over the rough terrain, more adept at handling sharp objects, determined to kill.

I stepped out with my Uzi. From the other side, Keilter Musselman joined me with an M240. We loosed another round. Neon blue filled the sky. In a way, it was like a dream come true. I felt like I'd just destroyed an entire nation's worth of flavored gelatin. But then came the acid rain. It went everywhere. The fizz and crackle of sizzling foliage filled the meadow. The screams of spattered men followed. The combination smelled like burnt macaroni.

More blue tarps showed up, men huddling together beneath them. Chantelle and I ran to another wide tree, our tarp becoming more and more threadbare. Only a few aliens remained, retreating into the hatch of their ship. That was the end of them. Or so I thought until a skinny arm grabbed my wrist, connected to a black earmuff-wearing alien.

I pulled back in alarm, but it had a solid grip. It pulled closer. "You defied us, but I will eat you and learn your secrets."

I pried at its multiple-suctioned fingers, to no avail. About to engulf my arm, its wet eyes went wide.

A sharp stick to the blob's side, Chantelle gave a wicked smile. "If you don't let go, you won't live long enough to even get a taste."

The blob released me, rotated its eyes to face

Chantelle, and lunged.

I slipped the tarp between us and the alien. Its bulging body still in motion, it pressed against the plastic, pushing us down, burning through. The poisonous stench filled my nostrils. Pressing the barrel of the Uzi against the tarp, between Chantelle and myself, I fired. We each rolled to one side, clinging to the tarp's edges as goop shot through the holes between us and splattered everywhere else. The middle of the tarp disintegrated, leaving little besides the seamed edge.

With a squelch like gelatin through a straw, the monstrous ship lifted off the ground, turned invisible, and was gone.

"Will you marry me?" I whispered in Chantelle's ear, careful not to drop to one knee.

We didn't tell the community what had happened. It rained that afternoon and the alien remains washed away. Without evidence, who would believe us? Stories of a very large, vicious, mountain lion became the local legend. Chantelle and I married. After finishing at BYU, I found a job that would let me telecommute. We built a house in Monticello, near the base of Blue Mountain. I kept a close eye on the area, always searching for any signs that the aliens might return. With the destruction of the orb, people's compulsions became manageable, but they still had to take the time to think about their decisions. Sadly, some didn't want to put forth the effort.

Gelatin became a very unpopular item at ward and community functions. Some people, mostly the rough, gun-toting men, cringed and shuddered whenever it jiggled in a 9 x 12 on the casserole side of the table. Sister Shumway and her family moved to a suburb of Salt Lake City where flavored gelatin was universally accepted. She couldn't understand people's sudden aversion to her favorite side-dish. The rest of us were happy to see her take the Jello and go.

Author's Note

"If you can't laugh at yourself, then how can you laugh at anybody else? I think people see the human side of you when you do that." ~Payne Stewart

"Obsessions" is me writing for fun. I spent much of my childhood in Monticello, Utah, where my father grew up, then I married a man raised for much of his life in the adjoining town of Blanding. I decided to set my story in a place of family heritage while poking a stick (pun intended) at some of the idiosyncrasies of Mormon culture. I'm LDS (Mormon), and like has been said many times and in many ways, if you can't make fun of yourself then you're not having enough fun.

False Reality

The second time my mom died I swore I would never put my own kids through the pain my parents had made me suffer.

It was summer, and like most twelve-year-old boys, I wanted to hang out at the pool. We didn't have one, but Jaron Lascano did. He stood in the living room with me, both of us tall and skinny, our swim shorts cinched tight at our bony hips. I stood an inch taller, my blond buzz a direct contrast to his black curly hair, and his skin a few shades darker, but we fought and played like brothers, until that day.

"Dad, I'm going swimming at Jaron's house," I yelled down the hallway. "I'll be home by dinner!"

It took Dad a second to respond. Like always, he was so wrapped up in his work that he didn't react right away.

"You have a dentist appointment this afternoon. You have to be home by two o'clock."

"Aaah, come on, Dad. That's barely an hour and a half. Serious?"

"I'm serious, David. You must be home for your mother to take you to the scheduled appointment."

Dad talked like such a nerd.

"Fine. Whatever. I guess I'll jump in the pool and come back."

"Make sure you're on time. You know how your mother hates having to come and get you."

"Yeah, I know."

Mom didn't mind getting me; it was going near a pool that bothered her. She and Dad both had some psycho fear of water that I didn't understand. I remembered my mom dropping me off at lessons until I'd taken every course the local pool offered. I figured she must have managed the shallow end at one point, because I had a vague memory of floundering near the stairs until she scooped me up and congratulated me for kicking. That was my favorite memory of my mother, the one I held onto.

Jaron and I barreled down the street of our Texan suburbia neighborhood, our towels streaming behind us like capes, flip-flops slapping the hot concrete. We wanted to make the most of the little time we had, so we went through the back gate and straight to the pool, dropping our sandals in the grass before shattering the clear water with our curled-up bodies, doing cannonballs. It seemed like we'd only been there ten or twenty minutes when I heard my mom's voice from inside the Lascano's house.

My eyes darted to the black and white clock hanging on the porch wall. "Crap! I'm so busted."

I climbed out of the pool, searching the grass for my sandals. Mom was going to be ticked about taking me to a dentist appointment in swim shorts and sandals. She always made sure I dressed in certain

115

types of clothes for certain things, as if she had a list. She probably did.

I searched the long grass, suspecting Jaron had skipped out on mowing this week. "Jaron, I can't find my other sandal."

Our sights landed on Ralph, Jaron's menace of a Labrador. Sure enough, he'd slipped through a newly-dug hole at the edge of his kennel. He lay under the Lascano's grapefruit tree, gnawing at something black and plastic.

"Ralph!" Jaron yelled. "You stupid mutt."

Ralph left off chewing the side of my shoe, perked his ears, grabbed it and ran. His thick tail wagged back and forth, showing his enthusiasm for the chase. I look back at it now, glad Jaron wasn't in the pool and that we were both running around the backyard like crazy people, trying to catch the stupid dog.

Ralph ran between us. Jaron and I both grabbed at fur, but he slipped from our fingers. Mom had just stepped past the porch, shielding her eyes as she scanned the yard.

Ralph dropped the shoe, his tail pumping with renewed enthusiasm at the prospect of finding a new friend.

You'd think the dog considered himself a stupid Chihuahua or a lap-dog. I picked up the remains of the black plastic as he catapulted into her arms. Mom hated dogs. Maybe it was Ralph's just desserts that he fell with her into the pool.

The splash surprised me, but not as much as what happened afterward. The water roiled and sizzled like bacon dropped onto an over-heated pan. Ralph yelped, whined, and went silent. Mom never made a sound.

Jaron and I ran to the edge of the pool. Mom lay at the bottom, glassy eyes staring at the diving board. Ralph floated toward the shallow end, a thin line of fur floating above the surface,

She'd only been down a few seconds. I'd taken all the lifesaving courses, including CPR. I could save her. I threw my arms out and dived.

Before I completed the jump, Mr. Lascano caught hold of me. He pulled me off my feet, backing us away from the pool.

"You, too, Jaron," he said. "Get away from there. The electricity will fry anybody who touches it."

Jaron followed his dad without hesitation, his eyes wide and disbelieving.

I struggled against Mr. Lascano's strong grip. "What are you talking about? Let me go! I can still save her."

He grabbed my skinny arms and turned me to face him. His grip bruised as I squirmed, but he forced me to look into his eyes. "She's gone, David. I'm sorry. The old trial units aren't as waterproof as the new ones."

"Units?" My resistance halted as little bits and pieces of the puzzle slammed into place inside my brain. "What do you mean, units?"

"They haven't told you yet?" He released one arm to wipe a hand over his face. "What were Bruce and Mellie thinking?"

"His parents are cybers?" asked Jaron. "How?"

I glanced back at my mother. She lay still, her clothes drifting in the pools small currents, almost obscuring the small black outline spread like a gun blast across the concrete bottom.

Memories rushed at me. I saw my mother, pale as the white diving board. Her head rested against the window of our car, blood running down her face, eyes staring forward. My dad had been worse. The pole that came off the back of the flatbed in front of us had impaled him, piercing through his chest, the seat, and partway through the back passenger door. Buckled in the middle, in a booster seat I'd nearly grown out of, I'd cried for someone to save them. And I thought they had.

"How old was I?" I asked Mr. Lascano. "When they died?"

He released my arms. "Four. Do you remember?"

I nodded. Mom and Dad had come home a couple of weeks later, looking the same as always. It had never occurred to me that there could be any other explanation. I had had nightmares for a while, but had considered them just that. Nightmares. But they'd been memories.

You'd think something would have triggered bigger questions before that point, but a guy just doesn't expect fake parents. I mean, maybe in Beverly Hills mansions, but not suburbia Texas. Finding out the Easter bunny, tooth fairy, and Santa weren't real hadn't come as much of a surprise, but my flesh and blood mom and dad...that was a shocker. Well, in my case, they were flesh, preservation fluid, titanium, a cpu, and some seriously advanced circuitry. What officially creeped me out, these cyber-parents were also, for real, my mom and dad.

A few minutes later, probably alerted to a malfunction, pseudo-dad arrived in the Lascano's backyard. It took nearly a full minute for him to process the events and come up with a response, but he finally turned dry eyes to me.

"We were programmed to tell you when you were

fourteen unless you asked specific questions or we experienced a malfunction. I guess the death of your mother qualifies."

"Ya think? What in hell are you?"

"Don't swear, David. Your parents arranged for cyber-parent creations in their will if functional units were available. Using your father's substantial inheritance, along with some assistance from the state's incentive program, they pre-paid for us. We cover our upkeep and your sustenance costs by operating as data storage devices and managing data entry for local companies."

"They left me to be taken care of by a stupid computer?"

Mr. Lascano placed a hand on my shoulder. "I'm sure they did what they thought—"

I knocked his hand off and stepped away. "You knew, but you let me believe, all this time, that they were real."

"I thought you knew, but you'd decided to act like they were real. I've heard some kids will do that. I never realized your parents programmed them to keep the truth from you. If I'd—"

"I am still real," cyber-dad interrupted. "This is your father's body. The bones were replaced with a state-of-the-art titanium structure, but the outer layer of tissue is kept fresh through an infused preservative system. As long as my head isn't immersed in water, my warranty won't expire for another eighty years. I've also received a memory, personality, and behavior-patterns download to ensure you are raised according to your father's wishes."

No wonder dad seemed a little too perfect sometimes. He was just some simulation, like artificial

119

color or a 4D movie.

Jaron stared at me with his mouth open, like I was the freak. He turned that expression on his dad, asking the question. "Are you—?"

"I'm real, son," said Mr. Lascano. "I promise."

I backed toward the gate. "This is wrong. This isn't fair!"

Dad stepped forward. "We need to get you to your dentist appointment. You're already ten minutes late."

I glanced back at the pool, waves of heat lifting from the black, oily surface. One of mom's systems must have sprung a leak.

My stomach heaved, but I kept the pool water down. I shook my head, turned, and ran.

Dad didn't follow me, so somehow Mr. Lascano must have convinced the thing to give me some time. I know the cyber-dad who raised me would have insisted I keep the appointment, dead mom or not. And in that moment, and every day since, I swore I would never do such a horrible thing to the people I love. If I ever died, I'd stay gone. I wouldn't haunt them by leaving a moving, talking, resemblance of myself behind.

Scott, my cyber-dad, never cried, of course. Life went back to its usual routine, only he took on Mom's tasks. He drove me to school and back. I started taking the bus. He made my lunches, but I started eating in the cafeteria and getting my own cereal for breakfast.

Jaron and I didn't talk about it. I avoided my former friend.

A few weeks later an insurance adjustor came to the door, confirming that her submersion in the pool was an accident then offering to replace Mom, but the policy would only cover a simplified version, with plastic casing. Her body had been fried too much to reuse anyway. Scott was going to take them up on it, but I refused. It was bad enough that I had to live with a cyber version of my father; I wouldn't have some stupid robot reminding me to wear clean underwear and brush my teeth. I didn't want a replacement for Mom, and if I could have, I would have shut down Scott. I probably could have killed him—fried his circuits like Mom, or bashed his head in—but I couldn't stand the thought of watching him die again, even if he wasn't real.

I choked back my tears, and we continued to live. Scott jacked into the wireless in one way, I jacked-in in another. Though he limited my computer time, every free moment not on the T.V. or my gaming system at home, I spent doing the same things at my friends' houses. Anything to block the pain, anything to block out reality.

At sixteen, I stole a car.

After pulling me over, the police officer shoved me against the side of the black BMW, yanked my arms behind my back, and tightened handcuffs around my wrists. "You're going down, boy. This isn't the kind of trouble you can just walk away from."

Though I shook with fear, I laughed in his face. "Hah. Maybe they can just butcher me up and make me into a nice cyber-boy, like everyone else in this stinking town."

The cop's digital eyes took a picture of me as he started reading me my rights, and I realized, he was a cyber-cop, part of the new initiative to cut down crime by putting more officers on the streets. Only these officers only required maintenance instead of pay and benefits.

Scott bailed me out, shaking his head as if he felt real disappointment. "David, why?"

I gave him a blank face, as devoid of real emotion as his own.

He took me to the juvenile system court hearing, standing ram-rod straight beside me, probably cataloguing data while he waited for the judge to get started. I slouched in my seat on a bench that was meant for both of us, a sullen expression hiding my racing heart. I'd heard stories about juvie. It made bad kids worse as much as it made any kid better. And things could happen to a kid who didn't know how to defend himself, a kid like me.

The proceeding started with a bunch of legal gibberish, mostly handled by my case-worker, some lanky guy I'd met five minutes ago.

"As this is a first offense," said the judge. "I'd rather not place David into a facility. However, stealing a car is a serious crime, as is the damage he caused to the interior."

My fake dad blinked a couple of times then spoke up, sounding as human as any person there, except for the lack of slang and the occasional missed contraction. "As you know, your honor, I'm a post-mortem, electronically-enhanced, cyber-human— model 24X-CY34. If you are willing to entrust David to my care, I can set security on our home which will ensure that he doesn't leave the premises without permission. He can have on-line school, do his work program, and be in lock-down for whatever specified time is deemed best without cluttering the overloaded juvenile facilities."

The judge breathed a huge sigh of relief, wiping her brow with a thick sleeve. "You cyber units are a godsend," she said.

I frowned, crossing my arms and moving to the far end of the bench.

She turned to the case-worker. "Is this amenable to you?"

The man nodded. I stopped listening. My fate was decided. It was better than jail, but a part of me had hoped to be rid of my fake father for a while. Now he would be my prison warden.

For six months, I saw counselors I refused to talk to, took online school, and learned how to hack Scott. I couldn't get away with re-programming anything too blatant. My time in detention had convinced me that I didn't want to go to juvie or any regular jail, so I kept it mild.

I got him to order pizza when I wanted. I fixed the security system so I could get out of the house once in a while. In the long run, the best thing that came out of it was Mr. Lascano spotting me walking home from a movie, well after curfew.

He flagged me from his front porch. "Hey, David. We haven't seen you for a while. Come on over."

He and Jaron sat in a couple of chairs, just hanging and shooting the breeze like they often did. The sight made me jealous, angry, but I didn't dare turn my back on them. If they reported me out late, I'd be playing the legal system again.

I stepped up the stone stairs onto the redwood front deck, my shoulders slouched, ready for the lecture.

"Have a seat," said Mr. Lascano. "It's good to see you moving around again. How're you doing?"

Surprised, I slunk down into one of the wicker chairs. "Fine."

He didn't say anything about my lock-down, my arrest, or any of the stupid things I'd done over the last few years, including slashing a few of his tires. We talked sports, school, and plans for our future.

"You know," he said, after telling us about a time he'd vandalized a school classroom, "I'm glad I didn't let all the screwy things I did as a teenager get in the way of my bigger dreams. I wouldn't have the family I have now if I hadn't put it behind me and strived for something better."

I could have taken the statement as a reprimand, but he was so sincere, talking about his own mistakes while letting Jaron and I know that he cared. Not just about his son, but about the neighbor boy down the street who used to hang out at his house and play in his pool. And for a moment, I felt like I really had a home, a place where I belonged.

❧❧❧

I started to let my guard down with the psych counselor. It took time, but she helped me get my head screwed on straight. Jaron and I became friends again, both of us ending up with scholarships at the same college.

We were hanging at the closest off-campus bar when I got a message on my sub-cu. I tapped the black disk in my ear.

I paused, my hand clenched around a half-full glass of beer.

"Something wrong?" Jaron asked, his own drink poised at his lips.

"Scott just messaged me." I said, staring at my reflection between bottles in the mirror. "He made the last payment to cover my room and board, and deposited all acquired funds into my account."

Jaron slapped me on the back. "Well, that's great isn't it? Your dad's taken care of you while you finish college and get a job." Jaron set down his drink. "What's wrong?"

I took a deep breath, keeping my voice steady. "As programmed, he notified the authorities to pick up his body and software, contacted me to say he'd fulfilled his contract, and shut himself down."

"Shut himself down?"

I took a long draft on my drink, wiping the foam from the stubble at my lip. "He's dead."

I slammed the glass to the counter, staring at my distorted reflection in the bar mirror.

Jaron didn't know how to respond. I couldn't blame him. What could he say? *But your dad is already dead. It's okay, he's not really your dad. Maybe you'll get some of the money when they sell off his ancient CPU and wiring.*

No, nothing could make the screwed-up situation with my father right. Nothing ever had.

I spun the thick glass between my fingers, waving the fake-brunette bartender toward me with the other hand. "Drinks all 'round on me." A chorus of whoops and cheers exhibited inebriated thanks. "I'm celebrating, so keep them coming for my friend and

I."

Jaron and I went to our apartment that night, drunker than we'd been in over three years. The next morning, my hangover nearly brought me to tears. But I had a class to T.A. There was no time to do anything but throw on a clean t-shirt, brush my teeth, and swallow a few aspirin as I stumbled out the door. I survived, my cyber-life finished.

A few years later I found a woman with similar goals who didn't mind my long hours at the office, who supported my Saturday golf meetings, and didn't complain when I had week-long conferences in Hawaii. By every measurement and every algorithm, we were perfect for each other. Three years into the relationship, she found out she was pregnant.

"It doesn't matter," she said. "I'll just abort the baby, and we can get on with our lives."

"No," I said. "I mean, I know that you can, but please don't."

I begged and pleaded with her throughout the entire pregnancy, always wondering if I'd come home to find her wearing a pencil skirt, our child in a biomedical disposal unit somewhere. I don't know why it was so important to me. Maybe because I felt like my parents abandoned me, maybe because I wanted to be the parent I'd never had, but despite her hate-filled glare, I cried when she brought our newborn son into the world.

Three weeks later, I found her packing boxes.

"I dissolved our lease," she said. "I've signed all the legal documentation, so Scott is entirely yours. I'm getting out of here."

With that, I became a single dad. Like everyone else in upper Manhattan, I hired a nanny. I wasn't about to leave my boy with some mechanical version of a babysitter. I wouldn't do what my parents had done.

Yesterday, eight-year-old Scott came tearing into my home-office, tears streaking his cheeks to the line of peanut butter smeared above his lip. Tearing his game controller from around his wrist, he threw it on the ground. It bounced, rolled, and came to a stop under my desk, rattling at my feet.

"I'll never get it! I can't figure out how to reach the stupid boss, no matter how many times I try."

"Stupid" had become his official adjective, adverb, noun and descriptor of choice for all things. I sighed, trying to keep my focus on the specs required for the software code I was writing. "Scott, you know you can't come in here when I'm working. Where's Chelsea?"

"She quit. Remember? When you told her she had to take me to those soccer games."

I did remember. I shouldn't have pushed the issue. Now Scott spent even more time glued to the latest Zbox than he did before. I eyed the fat bulging over the top of Scott's husky-size jeans. Still, he wasn't as big as Hansen's boy. That kid could eat three of Scott.

"Why don't you go outside, over to the playground?"

"I hate it there. It's all little kids and there's nothing to do."

"Isn't there a basketball court?"

"Our ball is flat. You said you'd fix it, but you're always too busy."

I scrambled around the house until I found the mini-compressor then fumbled around a little longer to find the right attachment. As the ball inflated, I accessed the time using my CIA—computer interface adaptor. It hung from the port I'd had installed behind my ear to replace my old sub-cu, over a year ago. The whole basketball process was taking twenty minutes. I could justify that as equivalent to a bathroom break and a glass of water.

I handed Scott the ball. "Okay, now get out to the playground for a while."

"With who?"

"Go find a friend or something," I said, using my CIA to access a message marked urgent.

I paused, listening to some flunky complain about his inability to understand the parameters for his assignment. I plugged another hour into my estimated completion algorithm and adjusted my schedule.

Scott still stood by the door, the basketball wrapped in both arms. "Will you play with me?"

"Look, I'm sorry," I said. "But I need to take care of this assignment. Maybe later, or tomorrow."

"Don't bother."

He chucked the ball. It bounced off the wall and nearly knocked over one of the lamps.

"Scott," I said, keeping my calm. "That is not acceptable behavior."

He shrugged, picking up the game controller he'd set on an end table. "So what? You'll go back to work and your stupid computer and won't even remember."

He headed toward the game room. "I'll just plug in and get the cheats. I can kill all those stupid cyber-people myself."

That comment jerked me upright, but Scott had left the room. For a moment, I thought he'd threatened me the way I'd mentally threatened my dad for all those years. But I'd kept to my promise. Even though cyber-nannies had become commonplace, I'd hired real people. And I'd spoken with Jaron Loscano and his wife; we'd drawn up a will that included adoption. If anything happened to me, Scott would be cared for by a family who could learn to love and care for him the way I did now.

Scott's words echoed in my head. I did care for him. I worked to keep him fed, taken care of, and I went to all of his games, when I could get a nanny who would take him to practice.

I took the stairs to my office two at a time, almost desperate to get back to work, but as soon as I stepped in my self-doubt stared at me from my image in the window.

Intending to shut the drapes so I wouldn't see my father's resemblance accusing me, I clenched the smooth, plastic frame and peered outside. My son's world came into stark focus.

Across the way, in an apartment identical to my own, a man sat at a desk-top managing his work with the same type of CIA as mine. In the room's opposite corner, a woman organized pictures and did mental typing, leaning back in her chair, using the same device. Toys sat in a neat box in the corner, but their two-year-old child sat in front of a 4D TV with a play-bracelet.

In the park next to the building, nannies circled the

playground where children fought with one another and cried, largely unheeded. Most of their caregivers, cyber and human, stared into space as they accessed their own sub-cu's and CIA's.

It reminded me of my childhood. Perhaps my cyber-parents hadn't been all that different from most of the humans, after all.

But then I remembered Jaron. His dad had actually taken him fishing. Once a year, every spring. Nobody did that, even back then. He hadn't enrolled Jaron in soccer, or music classes, or a whole lot of anything. But he'd played basketball with him in the driveway, soccer in the park, and gone swimming with us often. He'd shown up to Jaron's school activities and helped him with his homework. Sometimes, like the night he'd pulled me aside, they'd just sat outside their porch for hours, talking. I'd never felt as loved by anyone, not since my original parents died, as I did that night.

I glanced at my reflection again, the CIA sticking out of my neck. Despite all my promises, I'd become what I'd sworn I would never be. *I* was the cyber-parent. I wasn't like the mother who'd played with me at the local swimming pool. I was like the robot who had raised me.

I yanked the CIA from its port, unheeding the warning in my head that a storage device had been improperly removed and data might be lost. Closing the drapes, I returned to my desk.

For the first time in thirty years, I cried. My shoulders shook, great heaping sobs shaking my body.

The scuffle of small, heavy footsteps invaded my privacy. I didn't want Scott to see me like this, but I only managed to stop my heaving chest, and quiet the evidence of my guilt. The tears continued like a perpetual leak.

"Dad?" He took a tentative step inside. "Are you okay?"

I nodded my head, putting out my arms for the boy.

He hesitated, then ran into them, patting my back to give me comfort. I didn't deserve such a fine boy. Having looked out my window, I doubted many of us deserved the charges we'd been given.

"I'm sorry, son. I'll do better. I promise."

"Better at what?" asked Scott, pure innocence. "Did something get messed up at work?"

I choked back a laugh. Of course, he thought that was all that mattered to me.

"No, but there might be some problems soon. And that's okay. How would you like to live out west somewhere? Texas, maybe. How about Washington? There's probably some good fishing there."

"Why? Did you lose your job?" He pulled back in alarm. "Did I do something wrong?"

"It's not your fault. We're just going to make some changes. Maybe I'll get a different job. Might not pay as well, but it will be good for us."

"How? You've done your job for forever. What else can you do?"

I ruffled his hair. "I'm not a robot. I can change my programming. We'll figure it out."

Scott's frown deepened. "Are you okay?"

I took his hand in mine as we left the office.

"I wasn't, but I think I will be."

Author's Note

   "False Reality" didn't spend much time out in the submissions world finding a home, but it did spend enough time to earn an Honorable Mention from the Writers of the Future Contest during their 4th quarter of 2012. The story stemmed from my disgruntlement over the time my family spends with tech devices, and my desire to evaluate the quality of time that we give one another. This story makes me feel guilty, but I think it's a good kind of guilt, the kind that motivates us to try a little harder, and become a little more aware of what we're doing with this wonderful gift called life.

Demon River

Craydon stepped from rock to red-veined rock, occasionally forced to wade up to his knees, crossing the pink-hued Darklur River. He chuckled to himself, recalling the local legends. People would rather believe in demons and monsters than the simple, common truth; the red rock colored the clear waters to their unnatural taint. He could understand their uneasiness—the swirling color gave the impression he stepped through the diluted remains of an upriver murder—but he didn't share their superstition. A good man need not fear the conjured evils of simple minds. So his Da had always told him.

Drying his feet in the thick grass at the river's bank, Craydon set his damp gear in the sun to dry, selected a thick branch, and whittled it into a makeshift fishing pole. A piece of dirty string attached a struggling beetle to the wood, which he threw into the pink-tinged eddies as bait. He sat that way, finding new insectile victims when the former ones drowned, for nearly an hour.

As he pierced the body of another multi-legged creature and threw it in, Craydon decided this would be his last try. The shadows were lengthening and his pack was dry. A loud growl from his cramped stomach and a cluster of small fish disappeared under rocks and into clumps of river grass.

"Not again," Craydon grumbled under his breath, though not loud enough to spook more fish.

Sunlight glimmered red through the flowing water, the Darklur being one of few rivers in the north kingdom that lapped at its banks instead of struggling for enough width and depth to force a traveler to wet his feet. There was a splash, announcing a larger fish, but Craydon saw nothing except a small minnow darting among the rocks.

"There be no hope for a decent lunch now."

Leaning his large frame against a tree, he sighed deeply. In another day, he should reach home. Theydon and little Lilaine would run out to meet him. He missed their laughter. He especially missed their mother. Craydon smiled as he thought of Reane's golden hair, large blue eyes and small, inviting lips.

He patted the satchel on his back, contracts to sell his leather skills at the upcoming fair. Reane had grumbled some at having her husband gone for so long, but the trip had proved fruitful, with the added good fortune that the king had actually lowered taxes in light of the recent drought. They might have the means to purchase a few cattle, get a herd started.

He shifted on the rough ground, yawned and stretched. "Please little fishies. Couldn't just a one of you give me a little nibble so a poor hard-working man can have some food in his gullet?"

The line went taut. Craydon jerked the branch, lifting his prey from the river. "What in the names of the ancestors—"

A fleshy fish, about the size of his hand, poised above the clear waters, stuck to his hook as if already dead. Sparkling scales gleamed with the color of fresh blood except at its fins and tail, where the red darkened, giving the impression of a thick congealing scab. Its eyes bulged from its fat head like puss-filled blisters with a blackened clot for a pupil.

Craydon pulled the hook from its gaping mouth, prepared to throw the ghastly thing back into the river. His stomach growled, protesting the foolish notion. Throwing it back would serve no purpose, and that one fish would give him a full belly. Tales of the river whispered among his memories, but he pushed them aside. Local superstitions had no place for a hungry man.

Building a small fire, he placed a good cooking rock in the middle, making a woodsman's stove. The familiar scent of burning ash coiled in the air as he set about cleaning and cooking the fish.

It didn't take long to cook, and he picked the flesh off the warm stone. After consuming the last flake of meat, he gazed at the carcass—more eerie than when he'd pulled it off the hook. The intense eyes stared through him. In another fish, he'd have eaten the eyes and every bit of the head, not wasting a morsel. But not this one, its eyes like a blood-blister ready to burst.

He scraped the bones back into the stream. "May your spirit find rest and receive the blessings of a life given in service."

At first, the bones floated lazily down, toward the riverbed. Then they began swirling closer together, reassembling. Thin strands of cartilage attached themselves to the long, flexible vertebrae. The missing chunks appeared from the gurgling waters, connecting to their rightful places.

Craydon stumbled back. "By the ancestors!"

The skeleton swam to a rock at the bottom of the river. Devouring a school of small, silver minnows, it filled with blood and flesh, becoming whole again. It turned an uncanny eye in Craydon's direction. Flapping a bloody tail fin, it disappeared from sight.

Bone scraped his knife across the smooth stone a few more times, making sure the blade would cut sharp and quick. He liked the feel of a slick blade gliding through firm flesh, stripping away muscles and tendons.

He replaced the knife in the scabbard at his back. He held multiple knives: short, long, jagged, smooth, some visible, and others where no one would think to look. The call of a kyrtlebird pierced the air—two long trills then a short one. His head perked up—that was Tarren's signal.

Bone motioned to Farly, waving him down the hill. Then Bone slipped silently to the road's edge, hiding behind a stand of pines.

A big man with a thick neck, wearing drab farmer's garb, walked past with a knapsack over one shoulder, whistling a tune. The melody of *Sweet Miller Rine*, a children's ditty, floated toward them. A family man.

Bone's lip curled with contempt.

Farly stepped in front of the man, his knife drawn. A wicked grin spread across his face. "Excuse me, sir."

The man stopped, stepping back warily. "The name be Craydon Leatherwork."

"Well then, Mr. Craydon, I'm afraid I need to lighten your load some."

Bone hated the way Farly played genteel-like with their victims. It didn't get the right tone across. When Craydon turned to run, Bone was already there, his wiry frame blocking the path. "What he means is...you give us the stuff or we stick you." Bone twirled his knives.

Craydon paled. "T-take whatever you want. Pl-please just let me pass."

Bone pointed to the sack with one knife. "Real slow like. Take that off and throw it behind you."

Craydon threw the shriveled knapsack to Farly.

Tarren sauntered down the path to Bone, still singing like a kyrtlebird.

"Knock it off." Bone glared at him. "We're down to business here."

Bone handed Tarren a knife, gesturing for him to keep an eye on their captive. Bone approached Farly who had spread the sack's meager contents on the hard dirt. He flushed with rage.

"This all you've got? A few paltry herbs, some parchment, and ink? The only coin here is a couple of bronzes. Are you hiding the rest somewhere else? Did you see us afore you came up?"

Craydon trembled. "No. I swear I'm not hiding a thing. I didn't plan well for me journey. I ran out of food, spent most of my coin at the last village for a dinner so I be making it home. This is all I've got, everything I own."

Bone drew another knife. With a quick flick, a trickle of blood oozed from Craydon's cheek. "Bring 'im with us," Bone snarled.

Farly placed a knife at Craydon's back. Tarren settled one against his ribs. Each of them grabbed an arm.

"If'n I don't get the goods," said Bone, "I'll at least get some fun for my troubles."

"Please, take what I have and let me be." Tears filled Craydon's eyes. "I've got me a wife and children waiting. They be frantic with worry already, I'm sure."

"Well, we wouldn't want them worrying for no reason, now would we? Now they have a reason."

Bone laughed, gesturing for Farly and Tarren to take hold of the man. They dragged Craydon deep into the woods, far enough that no passersby would hear his screams.

Bone snickered as Craydon tried to suppress heavy sobs. But the crying got to Tarren. He kept darting nervous glances at Bone, obviously itching to say something, but not able to gather the nerve.

Fifty feet ahead, Bone found the tree he wanted. "Tie him up."

"Bone," Tarren finally spoke. "What's it matter? Why don't we let him go? He ain't got nothin' for us."

"Exactly, and I don't allow anyone to waste my time. He's at least gonna give me the pleasure of practicing my knives."

"But he's just a common man. I know we ain't been together long, but what be the point of knifing up a common man? He's not competition, a warning to others, or nothing."

Bone slashed his knife across Tarren's shirt, slitting it from chest to hip. "I suggest you keep your maw shut, or I might draw blood...on accident."

Tarren's fearful eyes stared at Bone's knife. He turned away, found an overturned log, and sat with his hands over his ears.

Farly pulled Craydon's arms back, securing him to the strong pine, then he and Tarren took sullen steps back to camp. Bone watched them, glowering. He knew they were getting restless with his leadership. But he didn't care. If he had to dispose of them, he could always find more. Men like them abounded in these hard times.

He turned back to the traveler, rotating his small, sharp knives. He already knew where to cause a man pain and he enjoyed experimenting with various methods; determining how far he could go before the killing. If he went too quickly, it would end too soon. He'd feel dissatisfied. Keeping the man conscious, screaming and pleading, provided infinitely more pleasure. Only towards the very end, when the man's agony was constant, his nerves screaming pain, mind still coherent, would he cut deeper into the flesh. He wanted the man alive, still aware, when he began removing the organs from his bowels and chest. The process required delicacy and patience. Men passed out too easily.

Bone pressed the flat of the blade softly against the man's cheek. Wet tears christened the metal.

"Please...no," Craydon cried.

Bone angled the knife gingerly against the muscled chest, panicked breathing making it heave and quiver. Blood pooled. He pressed harder. His prey screamed. Bone laughed and proceeded, piece by fleshy piece.

By the time he'd finished, Craydon's skeleton hung limp against the blood-soaked tree. Around them, bits of clothing mingled with red-tinted mud and wet pine needles.

Washed up and clean, Bone sat on a tree stump in front of the evening campfire. Tarren and Farly sat across from him, using a fallen tree as a bench. When an animal scampered deep in the bushes, they jumped, reaching for knives.

"There's nothing out there," Bone said. "You act like scared little girlies. What's wrong with you?"

They glanced at one another. Farly fidgeted with a twig. "That stranger was coming from Demon River. It's a two-day walk from the last village where he could have spent his money on a meal. When he passed by me, he seemed quite happy for someone who hadn't eaten in two days."

Tarren nodded, white with fear.

"So what?" said Bone. "Mebbe he done found something to eat along the way."

"That's what we be afraid of," said Tarren.

"We're not getting into that again, are we? There ain't no demon killer fish. That's crazy talk—an old wives tale."

Farly shook his head. "I'm telling you, Bone. My last band got wiped out from eating a Blood Fish. Being the youngest recruit, I was the last to eat. That's the only reason I'm alive. O'course, by the time I got my share, I didn't want it. While they screamed, holding their bloated bellies, I watched the skeleton of that fish wiggle off to the river and put itself back together. Fish just like it, fat with new flesh, crawled from the mouths of each of the men who ate it. I saw it with

140

my own eyes."

"If'n that were true, our stranger would have been dead afore he ever reached us."

"I heard, if'n one was pure," said Tarren, "with no hate inside, then instead of killing 'ya, it protects 'ya. It turns them people into avenging monsters."

Bone laughed. "How's it going to get me if it's already dead? There ain't no vengeance from a dead man, and I ain't afraid of no ghostly spirits. There ain't nothing in existence that don't go down with a good knife in its throat."

Bone twirled one of his blades between his fingers. An animal rustled the bushes behind him. He turned, in hopes of seeing a rabbit or maybe even a deer. It'd be nice to add some meat to the fire.

Craydon emerged from the darkness on fractured legs. His bulging, dead eyes stared ahead. Naked and covered in dry blood, most of Craydon's flesh had been stripped clean. His abdominal cavity was disemboweled clear to the spine. The only organ not maimed was his drooping heart. It hung where his stomach should have been, still beating.

As Tarren and Farly watched, the nightmare closed the distance between himself and Bone. He thrust his skeletal hand through Bone's flesh, deep into his abdomen. Bone screamed.

The two henchmen shot into the woods, tripping over branches and their own feet, but scrambling back up and running for the deepest, darkest places they might hide.

Bone stuck Craydon with his knife. There was no liver, but he pierced the drooping heart.

With his left hand, Craydon pulled the knife free. He dropped it to the dirt, reached his hand higher into

Bone's ribcage. He found what he sought in the upper, left side—the pulsing heart.

Bone struggled to break free.

Craydon's grip was like iron. His hand wrapped around the base of Bone's sternum. Cartilage snapped. Bone gasped for breath as a broken rib pierced his lungs. Blood gurgled in his throat. Writhing in pain, he cried for release.

Craydon yanked, ripping Bone's heart from his chest. Arteries still attached, it convulsed. Bone stared in horror. Craydon brought the warm heart to his lips. He took a bite.

Bone twitched. His eyes rolled up in his head as he went still.

Blood dripped between Craydon's fingers. He licked at it hungrily. His damaged heart fell to the ground. Reaching into the corpse for another organ, he continued his feast.

Bit by bit, the flesh he consumed restructured into healthy organs and tissue. Craydon gnawed away clinging scraps of muscle, but the man was too small to fill his needs. Eventually, the bones crunched between Craydon's newly formed teeth. He sucked the marrow into his living body. He smirked at what remained of Bone's carcass, lying next to the smoldering fire.

With glazed eyes, his naked body drenched in blood, Craydon left the campsite whistling the light-hearted melody of *Sweet Miller Rine.*

Craydon staggered into the clearing, wide-eyed and confused. He had just enough sense to rip off a large Pellen leaf and cover his privates before his children caught sight of him.

"Papa!" Theydon cried, running toward him, arms outstretched.

Lilaine showed more caution, her approach more wary.

Theydon wrapped his wee arms around Craydon's stooped neck. He returned the boy's embrace with one hand, feeling whole for the first time since he'd crossed that bloody river, yesterday...two days ago? He still wasn't sure.

"What happened to yer, Pa?" Lilaine said, keeping a distance.

"Don't rightly know. I ate myself some fish I caught, was headed home, then the next I knew I woke up back in the river, water washing over me so I could scarce breathe." He set Theydon aside, standing up again. "I must have blacked out again, 'cause next I knew I be coming down yonder hill to home."

He glanced down at the leaf, barely doing its job. "Run in the house, there 'Lainey. Get your Ma to find me some clothes. Even if ya are my kin, this be a mite embarrassing, standing in the yard in me shivers."

She smiled a bit, some of the concern easing from her eyes and forehead. "Yes, Pa. I be right back."

She took off to the house—a small square of logs and mud-paste—her homespun gray dress rustling round her knees.

Craydon took his son by the hand, his other holding the leaf, and they followed Lilaine. When Reane burst from the door, hugging him as if he'd come back from the dead, he almost forgot about decency. More than anything at that moment, he would have liked to hold her close, take her onto their little bed in the cabin's corner, and show her how much he'd missed her.

But, of course, the children still stood waiting, their fearful eyes wondering about what had happened to their Pa, and what it all might mean. After all, they had grown up with the same tales he had, only they were more inclined to believe in them. Their concerned faces tugged at his heart, and he wanted very much to reassure them he was okay.

"I'd best get some britches on, then I'll tell y'all everything I can remember."

He took the brown bundle from Lilaine's arms, scooted through the door into their little house, and closed them out. A minute later he opened it again on their frightened, questioning faces.

"Come, now," he said. "It ain't all as bad as that, is it? I be home, all in one piece, and I have the contracts in me satchel. We'll have food for another year and maybe have enough to buy a couple of cattle. Gather up yer smiles, would ya?"

Theydon and Lilaine were quick to respond, but Reane's eyes weighed heavy with worry. "What happened to ya?"

"Like me told 'Lainey, I don't right know, but all feels right. I be fine, now. No worries to be had."

Reane's heavy sigh told Craydon otherwise.

"What happened whilst I was gone?" he asked.

"The constable raised our taxes. Even with the contracts, we ain't going to make enough without selling a part of our land again."

"That can't be right. Even on hard times, we done paid more than enough to meet the king's settlement. I even done heard that the king lowered the taxes, in light of the drought and all."

Reane whispered, as if someone might overhear. "There's rumor the constable has kept part of the taxes to himself. He's built himself a brand new house, over in the outskirts of town, on the land he took from Belervy."

Craydon ran a hand through his hair. "I'll go have me a talk with Basserdon Constable. See what be the truth."

Reane grabbed his arm. "People did that already. Some come back mad, but others don't come back. I want me husband more than I want a stitch of dirt."

"That stitch of dirt keeps food in our bellies. My leatherwork can only take us so far until we get cattle and make our own goods. We need that land if'n we're to feed the cattle, and we need our money if'n we're to ever buy the brutes to begin with. This thievery has gone on long enough."

With a gasp, Reane stepped back, a hand to her mouth. "Your eyes…"

"What?"

"They turned red," said Lilaine, her little brow furrowed. "But now they be right again."

Craydon thought of the fish, but cast his worry aside. "I be fine." He turned toward town, a two hour walk. "I'll be home in the morning."

Reane reached out and touched his shoulder. "But—"

"Stop yer worrying," he said, pulling her hand round his back and wrapping her into an embrace. "I feel better than a Spring colt, stronger than a she-bear. Basserdon won't give me trouble none."

He bent over and gave her a long kiss, making sure she understood just how refreshed and alive he felt, and how much he anticipated coming home.

She slipped a few coins into his hand. "I'll not have ya hungry and sleeping on the street."

He nodded then walked from the house to the fields. As he jogged between rows of dirt waiting for planting, she called out. "Be careful!"

But Craydon didn't need care. A fire burned in him like he'd never felt before. He needed justice.

❧❧❧

When Craydon entered the dirty little office, Constable Basserdon sat behind a Vettletree desk so shiny and new, Craydon could almost catch his reflection in the lacquered wood.

The man's smile was almost as slick as his desk. "Craydon Leatherwork, I heard you'd be home soon. I trust your trip was profitable?"

He almost growled. "You know I don't like yer small talk and fancy ways, Basserdon. Yer family comes from the same country stock as the rest of us out here. Before yer name was Constable, it was Pigmeat."

The practiced smile flipped to a sneer. "That's why some of us put forth the effort to move up in the world. I no longer raise pigs, nor does my family butcher them. My heritage will be gone and forgotten before my children ever knew it existed."

"But there'll always be folks like me who remember," Craydon said, enjoying the other man's glare. "But that ain't why I'm here. I want to know how you be cheating the books to take more from us farmers than you're allowed so you can stick the extra in your money-purse."

The constable slammed his hand against the wood,

but he saw the flash of fear that came before the anger. "How dare you accuse me of such a thing! You have no proof save your unwillingness to put in your fair share."

"I have no proof yet, but I've been to Teirken City. The king didn't raise no taxes, he lowered them. News is in every major port and city in the whole realm. And I be making sure everyone in the province knows it, and then you won't get a pit in your coffers, let alone a coin. What'll happen then, Pigmeat?"

Basserdon clenched his fists, eyes wild with murder. But for once, Craydon didn't fear what this man, with all his power and cunning, could do to him. He anticipated it. He pushed it.

"The duke'll be sending a report to the king," Craydon said. "The king'll find himself one of them accounts men. With soldiers and spies, the accounts man will come to look at our province, the money books, and the constable. What will he find, Pigmeat?" He paused, watching the man's desperation grow. "Or should I be saying, Villagethief? That'll be what ya leave yer children for their name after the king be done with ya."

He reached for the door handle.

"I'll repeal your taxes," Basserdon said, his desperation making his voice raise a pitch. "You won't have to pay a cent."

"If'n I don't tell?"

"Yes," said Basserdon with relief, as if he didn't dare refuse.

As if considering, Craydon cocked his head. "I'm not thinking that be a good way to treat me neighbors." He wrapped his hand round the doorknob. "Now, if ya be excusing me. I have a lot of folks to talk with."

The constable rose from his desk, hands splayed across the cluttered surface. "You open your mouth, and I have men who will close it for you, permanent-like."

Craydon laughed. "I be counting on it." Over his shoulder, he stared the smaller man in the eye, feeling red rage burn over his skin. "But know this. The man who holds the knife be more accountable than the knife itself. It be on him, I'll take me justice."

"Is that a threat, Craydon Leatherwork? From the man who's never stood up to a fight in his entire life?"

"That would be depending on you."

Craydon only had to walk across the street to be at his place for the night. Peterdon Innkeeper kept a nice bar and boarding house that didn't cost a man too much. Craydon took a seat, ordered himself some mutton and biscuits, and realized how long it had been since he'd eaten. He spent enough of his coin on two more helpings that he didn't have enough left for a bed. Peterdon would have let him have it anyway, but he had a feeling it wouldn't be necessary. On impulse, he went for a walk.

It hadn't taken Basserdon long to put together his assassins. He'd silenced men before. They came at Craydon in the first alley he crossed.

"You there be the Craydon Leatherwork?" The lead among them spoke with such a strong southern accent that even having traveled the kingdoms to find business, Craydon had trouble understanding.

"Yer know I be him."

He let the men drag him into the dark recesses of the alleyway, back where the stench of dumped chamber pots and rotting garbage came to a foul peak.

The fear that hadn't touched him before suddenly blossomed in the pit of his full stomach. "Please, don't do this. I have me a family. A wife and two kids."

"Sorry," the man said. "This here be the only of the jobs I can find."

The two thugs behind him pushed him to his knees.

"Make it quick then," said Craydon.

The man's shoulders slumped. "Sorry I also be, but I must do it as my employer does demand."

With that, he stuck his knife in Craydon's neck, his arms, and his legs, careful not to sever anything that would make him die too quickly, but letting his heart pump his life out onto the putrid street. When Craydon's eyes rolled up into his head, darkness closing in, he felt the last plunge of the knife, into his heart. The man turned him on his side, blood pouring from multiple wounds, drenching him as it pooled. Then all went black.

⁂

"Basserdon," Craydon whispered.

His pale corpse stood above Basserdon as the man snored.

In a pink negligee that could only be ordered from the city at great expense, the constable's wife slept curled against the opposite edge of the thick mattress. Was it because she wanted as far from her husband as possible, or did she just feel more comfortable, isolated and huddled in her own space?

149

Craydon wrapped his cold hand over Basserdon's mouth.

The man's eyes flew open.

Once they widened and his body jerked in fearful protest, Craydon knew the constable recognized him in the window's pale moonlight.

A withered finger, the skin and muscle tight to the bone like a starved calf, thrust between the startled man's ribs. Through skin and tissue, it pierced Basserdon's pumping heart. He convulsed, tried to scream, but Craydon held him tight, muffling the sound.

The wife stirred, but remained fast asleep. Reane would have never slept through such violence in their bed.

Craydon rotated his finger, expanding the hole. It squelched as he unplugged the wound, wet tissue clinging to his finger. As soon as he put his mouth to the reservoir, quietly sucking Basserdon's life to fill the void in his own flesh, the man lay still.

His wife didn't stir again until after he left through the open window. Several minutes later, a scream pierced the quiet night.

The approach of horses tromping along the dirt road edging Craydon's field tore him from the comfortable void of monotonous work. He stopped his hoeing and looked up. Soldiers, dressed in the king's colors of blue and silver, escorted a man wearing the rich colors and tight weaves of a nobleman. The hoe gripped tight, he strode between rows of radishes, carrots, and seedling melons to intercept the men before they reached his homestead. If something were to happen, it would be best away from Reane and the children.

Craydon stepped into the path moments before the lead soldier's horse. For a moment, he thought the man might run him down, but the soldier reigned in and peered down his nose as if he were the nobleman.

The soldier struggled with his horse, which tried to sidestep away from Craydon, nostrils flaring and eyes spooked. "Move out of my way, peasant."

"There's nothing this way but me homestead. Perhaps ye be searching for another path."

The nobleman dismounted his horse, which was the only one standing steady.

"Are you Craydon Leatherwork?" the nobleman asked, eyes bright.

"Yea, sir. That be me."

"It seems there's been some unrest in the town, most of it pointing to you."

"And ye be?"

"Ah, excuse me for missing the formalities." He made an elaborate bow, swishing his triangle cap from his head and stirring up dust as it brushed past his feet and back again. "I am Duke Derkensen, your liege lord and humble servant to the king."

Craydon had learned enough in the city, to know when to show respect. He dropped to one knee and bowed his head. "How may I be helping, sir duke?"

"Please, stand. Such subservience is unnecessary."

Craydon came to his feet, staring down at the smaller man.

The duke paused, evaluating him as if looking for a clue, some twitch that might give him away. "It seems you caused some unrest telling the locals about the king's decree to lower taxes. When the constable was murdered, the king sent me and a few of his soldiers to look into matters."

"I done heard ye be coming, but what need have yer with the likes of me?"

"It seems the constable was milking the books, stealing, and he didn't like your interference. The night the man died, villagers found a pool of blood in an alley, as if someone stuck a man and let him bleed out."

"That be a horrible way to go."

"Yes." The duke scratched at his chin. "Thing is, no corpse. All that blood, and not a body to be found...except, they discovered the constable, withered up like the shed skin of a fenske snake, not a drop of blood in him and only a hole, pierced into his withered heart, to show how the man might have died."

"That be right strange," said Craydon, unsure what response the man expected.

He remembered being cornered in the alley, and he remembered walking in the road outside Basserdon's home, the taste of blood in his mouth and a smear of it caking his neck and clothes. He'd walked away, whistling *Sweet Miller Rine*, until he'd come to himself, puked behind a tree, and scrubbed himself raw in the closest river, getting off the blood--real and imagined.

"At first I thought maybe a strange animal had infested the town," said the duke. "But upon further study, decided the culprit was human. Don't get me wrong. I was glad to leave the responsibility of Basserdon's justice in someone else's hands, but I wanted to meet you, be sure for myself that you hadn't murdered him out of some sense of spite, coming for the man's blood...literally."

"Basserdon be deserving of spite, but I ain't never attacked a man to get at revenge. Ain't my way."

"No, I can see that." The duke stared straight into his eyes. Craydon couldn't tear his gaze away. "I think you may be the kind of man who demands justice, but never revenge."

Something inside flared, a hunger he knew would never be satisfied, not until the day he grew old and died. "Justice," he agreed, tasting the word as a hungry man tasted an imagined feast.

The duke nodded. "We'd like to hand over the keeping of the law to you. Your name will be Craydon Constable, if that is amenable."

The soldier, still fighting his horse, gasped. "A peasant? Sir, are you sure—?"

The duke's eyes flashed. "I'll deal with you later."

And Craydon understood. For the briefest moment, the duke's whites turned blood red. The color of the Demon River fish. The color Craydon's wife had seen flash in his own eyes. The color of the blood he'd drained from the Constable. His memory of the event came back, full force.

Sickened, he sought to turn away. Yet even as he condemned himself and the duke, he saw inside the soldier's soul. He saw the man's joy at causing pain, the injustices he'd forced upon others, the humiliations he'd considered the due of those below him, and he saw the murder the young man had already committed. He saw what the soldier would do when the duke cornered and accused him, and he saw how the soldier would die.

Craydon knew his eyes flared to match the duke's, the desire for justice burning at his belly. The horses whinnied and shied farther away, nearly dumping two of the soldiers. But the duke's steed remained stalwart as stone. It waited upon its lord and master, accustomed to his inhuman scent—the slight tang of river water and bloodfish.

"Will you accept the call?" the duke asked.

Craydon nodded. "There be a condition."

"Yes?"

"If ever I be wrong, ye will mete out justice on me."

The duke nodded. "I will. But trust me, you will never err. It's not in you."

"If I have no mercy then I be worse than them men I might be sent to punish. I'll be having the greater sin."

"Mercy has no part in justice. If the crime is in a man's heart, then the crime must be returned."

"But what if the man knows he done wrong, feels sorry for it?"

"It's too late."

Craydon shook his head. "I be not your man."

In a single stride, he gripped the soldier's reigns in one hand, pulled his sword from its sheath with the other.

Before anyone could react he rotated the pommel and with all the force of his bulging muscles, shoved the sharp point into his own chest. Through his sternum and out his back, he felt nothing more than a pinch and a familiar drain. He'd already died twice. This didn't compare. He fell face down in the dirt.

The duke knelt beside him, letting peasant's blood coat the knees of his breeches. "When you feel better, the post is yours. The keys to the Constable's house are in the top drawer of his office desk."

"Why did he do that?" the soldier said, his voice

reaching Craydon as if from a far distance. "Was he the murderer?"

"No, he's a much better man than that. A much better man than I, in fact. By the end of the day, Alfren, you'll wish that I were such a man. This constable will understand mercy. A concept, I'm afraid, I find completely foreign. We'll discuss it, shall we, after we make camp and have had some dinner?"

They rode away, the duke's melodious rendition of *The Blessed Adeleide* drifting softer and softer until Craydon Constable passed out and died.

It was not the first time, nor would it be the last.

Author's Note

Among my critique readers, this seems to be a universal favorite. It was accepted by a magazine for publication in April 2013, but the magazine changed ownership, missed their promised publishing date, and didn't contact authors about the problems until afterward. I decided to take their offer to terminate the contract with payment, which they didn't follow through with either. Needless to say, I won't submit to them again, but my tragedy is also our reward. Because it missed getting published, I was able to include it in this anthology.

Acknowledgments

A lot of people have been there for me throughout my writing years. My husband has supported me one-hundred percent. He's kept me going when I doubted my right to spend so much time and money on something so questionably profitable. My kids have been instrumental, each in a different way, to making this happen.

Gini Koch has mentored me and encouraged me from the day we met on an airplane headed to San Jose for a writing convention. I will forever be grateful to her for telling me my first story was crap, and then telling me not to give up. Glen Glenn served as my critique partner for many of my stories, sharing his insights and corrections. Many of these stories were also vetted by members of the *Queen Creek Author's Association*. Thanks guys and thanks for all the *Paradise Bakery* cookies (I think). A number of my friends from Superstars Writing Seminars also gave me critiques and suggestions. Without them, I never would have had the courage to put this anthology together.

A special thanks and a few hugs go out to Quint Seymore--artist, friend, and excellent *Magic the Gathering* player--for his enthusiasm as he put together the cover and interior sketches. His talent continues to develop, and continues to astound me.

Last, but not least, thank you to friends and fans. I kept the stories in my mind for so many years. Thank you for encouraging me to finally share.

About the Author

Colette Black lives in Arizona with her husband, five kids, two dogs, and a cat. She enjoys being outdoors, traveling, and reading. She writes during all the rare moments between chaos.

For more information, go to: www.coletteblack.net

Noble Ark (available now)

"All civilians, lock up inside quarters." The computer's calm voice projected through all intercoms, as if trying to negate the horrors about to happen. "Sectional forcefields commencing in thirty seconds. This is your final warning."

Alarms blared through the corridors, reverberating against the thin metal of interior bulkheads. Outside, automatic turrets fired a few more useless rounds at the invading vessel. The *Noble Ark*, though a solid merchant transport, wasn't equipped to slow a Mwalgi craft of the caliber giving chase.

Aline glanced out an overhead observation window, angling so she could see the ship alongside. Matching the *Noble Ark's* speed, the black arms of the Mwalgi vessel latched onto various passenger portals like snakes clasping their prey. Metal clanged against metal outside the docking portal fifty meters from her position.

She shivered. Not much longer now.

Her bulky acid gun tight against her torso, she leaned against a defense pillar. The laser sighting shone a pinpoint of red light on the side wall, wavering back and forth with Aline's heavy breathing.

She held the firearm more for comfort than protection. It remained useless until the Mwalgi pirates—filthy Gi—smelled flesh and brought down their bodyshields. In two minutes, they'd reach the interior hatch. Another five to ten and they'd torch through the heavy bolts holding it closed. When they swarmed the corridor, Aline would be running for her life, firing acid pellets to slow the frontrunners.

When she'd first learned to use a gun, at eleven years old, the sight of the alien Mwalgi bursting onto a ship had petrified her. Even hiding in the ventilation shafts, watching, Aline had clutched her weapon with sweaty hands, praying to some unknown deity for survival. That time was gone. Those emotions no longer existed. She'd learned to suppress the fear, channeling her hatred into hard determination.

Tapping the communication disk behind her ear, she reconnected to the main battle frequency, listening to the conversations transformed from thought into words.

<*Bait crew in position, sir,*> a voice sounded in her head.

<Acknowledged,> Eric Mull responded. Sokan Mull, she corrected. If she was ever going to convince them to treat her like military, she needed to use rank instead of first names. *<First and second lines of resistance are in place. You know what to do.>* Mull's voice deepened, the software managing to convey an edge of embarrassment. *<Has anyone seen Captain Trenoble's daughter, Aline Taylor? She's not responding to him. Has she snuck in among any of your units again?>*

For a man of Mull's rank—he was a sokan, for firsters' sake—he worried like a planet-bound girl.

Aline scanned the end of the corridor.

The expected pink light of a Mwalgi torch shone through the metal near the floor. The Gi had started cutting the bolts, making their way in. The glow's slow upward movement remained steady, the sign of an experienced welder.

<Second-Lieutenant David Blake.> Mull sub-toned the name like an insult. *<Respond.>*

<Sokan Mull,> David answered, slurring the words with equal distaste. Even in sarcasm, his tenor voice dulled by automated translation, it made Aline breathe a little faster.

Mull paused. *<Well, have you seen her?>*

This was it. By regulation, David should tell his sokan everything he knew. But if he kept his word, he'd keep his mouth shut.

<I passed her in the corridor, sir. I assumed she was headed to merchant Tanaka's quarters, but when I checked later, I only found some refugee brat she'd sent over for safekeeping. I have no idea where she is, sir.>

David snapped every "sir." Aline could imagine spit flying into Mull's hair had the two men been face to face. She kept telling David that defiance wasn't the way to win over a commanding officer, but he insisted the only way he'd get Sokan Mull to like him was to die. Men could be so stupid.

<If anybody sees her, bring her to me immediately,> Mull sub-toned. *<The captain's going to have her spacesuit for this.>*

He always said that. Aline imagined the firsters, fresh from Earth, had talked like Mull did. If they'd had any idea a millennium ago what their descendants would be up against, would it have made a difference? Would they still have come, knowing parasitic aliens would plague them for centuries? Despite the casualties the firsters had already suffered, maybe they would have searched a little farther for a habitable planet instead of settling on Saeana.

The pink dot at the end of the corridor had moved a third of the way up the door, charring the metal.

Mull pinged her private comm line for the billionth time. Would he just stop already? Ark—Captain Trenoble, she corrected herself— might be upset now, but when she succeeded, he'd be proud.

A second later, David tried.

Aline tapped the disk behind her ear. *<Second-Lieutenant Blake?>*

<Come on, Aline, drop the titles. We're PCs, not space military. And you're not even accepted to Space Training yet, let alone signed up with the Private Contractors Association.>

<I should be.> Aline responded. *<The space training age restrictions are stupid. I finished top of my class and graduated from flight training early. You'd think that would be enough. Back on Earth, people used to enter the military at eighteen! I'm a year older than that.>*

Aline wiped sweaty palms against her grey-blue shirt, pausing as she remembered Commander Harris doing the same thing. She tucked the gun under one arm, reached into her pocket, and pulled out a small tube, listening to David as she worked.

<They didn't have to learn about space travel or pass low-gravity tests, and that was over a millennia ago."

<But—>

<Look, Aline, I told you I'd talk to my dad and help you get past the admissions board. You shouldn't try to fight without some backup.> David sounded as worried as Mull. *<Where are you?>*

She bristled at his condescending tone. Aline may have been younger than him, but she had more experience and training than he realized.

Squeezing gel into her left palm, she worked it methodically through her short hair, greasing the spiky ends--a little insurance in case she ended up in hand-to-hand combat with the Gi. If she could have, she'd have greased her entire uniform.

The Mwalgi torch approached the curve at the top of the door.

<Stay at your post,> she told David. *<You need to remain with your assigned commander or you'll be in deep reactor sludge.>*

She wiped the remaining goop onto the thighs of her matching pants, the same way Harris had, leaving darkened splotches. Gi invaders had killed Harris in the last raid. The gel trick hadn't helped her much. Aline shook the memory from her mind.

<Something could happen.> David's concern sounded genuine. <I want time to get to know you, Aline... really get to know you. Just stay out of this one.>

Could he really be interested in her? It didn't seem possible. David was easily the most gorgeous man she'd ever seen. Why would he look twice at a nineteen-year-old orphan from nowhere?

<I'll be fine.> She gripped her gun tight, watching the pink dot reach the top of the hatch. <Did you find a place for my extra pellet canisters?>

<Yeah, I've got them right here.> He sounded relieved.

David seemed to think she didn't want to carry extra pellets because she wouldn't need them behind the lines, but in truth, they'd only get in her way. Acting as bait required she be quick and agile. If she succeeded at getting the Gi to drop their shields early, the Saeanan forces could converge on them before they came anywhere close to the civilians, and then she'd be able to retrieve her extra canisters. If she failed... well, then she'd be dead. It wouldn't matter how much ammunition she carried.

<Who's supposed to bait?> Aline asked, more to calm her nerves than anything else. She didn't want to think about what would happen next. Not yet.

<On our deck? Lieutenant Brin Rachs and Jang Clarin Murphy. Why?>

<When the bait guys fall back, I'll be with them.>

David's thoughts spluttered, translating through the line as faint static. <But that means... you can't. Not by yourself.>

<If I get into trouble, or if it's more than I can handle, I'll tap my comm and you can come save me.>

<Have you seriously gone beyond our front line, beyond the bait team even? Are you crazy?>

The faint dot had gone past the curve, halfway down to the ship's deck again. Not much longer now.

David tried one last tactic. <By Saeanan space law, it's illegal for you to fight. Since the war started, only personnel with military training are allowed to operate or defend a space vessel. You need to come back.>

Aline rolled her eyes, though he couldn't see her. <I have military

training. It's just not formal *training.>*

The Mwalgi welder had less than half a meter to burn.

She took a deep breath. *<Gotta go. It's almost time.>*

<But—>

She tapped the disk, cutting him off.

She hated the last couple of minutes before a fight. The silent wait made it hard to keep her nerves steady. She could do this. And if she pulled it off, the admissions board might finally let her enlist, without David's help.

She checked her vacuum-sealed ammo chamber for the third time. It held a large supply of bright red pellets in a long cylindrical tube attached to the gun's narrow barrel, similar to the water guns she'd played with back at the Honor Corps Academy, only much sleeker. She'd been sent there a couple of years after her family died.

Memories of her mother, father, Tara, and Garrik pushed into her mind despite her determination to keep the past boxed away. The way they'd all screamed, and the blood… there had been so much blood. They were gone. She had no family, no one to leave behind. Revenge was her only purpose.

She tightened her focus, stuffed away the thoughts. Melancholy and fear could play in the shadows of sleep. Her current opportunity promised retribution. And they would pay. All the Mwalgi would pay for their centuries of human murder.

The walkway lights dimmed. They would still reflect off the Mwalgi's silvery scales, but with less glare.

The sirens stopped their angry wail. For the moment, all was still.

Aline stared at the dark metal doors.

The dull pink light completed its path.

Sweat rolled down the back of her neck, soaking into the short collar of her form-fitting uniform. She leaned forward.

The heavy door screeched, emitting sparks as it scraped across the deck.

She steadied her gun, balancing on the balls of her feet. She had to get close enough that they smelled her, close enough to arouse their bloodlust so they'd let down their bodyshields. Then she had to get out… fast.

The twisted, metallic remains of the door stopped a third of the way open. A large, muscled arm reached out, pushing the small, mangled remnants aside.

She adjusted her weapon, moving it out of the way. It wouldn't do any good until they caught her scent.

As the first beast appeared, she rushed forward.

www.ingramcontent.com/pod-product-compliance
Lightning Source LLC
Chambersburg PA
CBHW060425130626
46555CB00005B/2217